THE DISTANT STRANGER

Palma Harcourt was born in Jersey, where she now lives, and educated at St Anne's College, Oxford. Later she worked in various branches of British Intelligence, travelling widely and living in several capitals round the world. Her experiences have provided her with background material for her thrillers with diplomatic settings.

Also by Palma Harcourt:

PALMA HARCOURT

The Distant Stranger

Futura

A *Futura* Book

First published in Great Britain in 1984
by William Collins Sons & Co Ltd

This Futura edition published in 1985
ISBN 0 7088 2651 2
Reproduced, printed and bound in Great Britain by
Hunt Barnard Printing Ltd, Aylesbury, Bucks.

Futura Publications
A Division of
Macdonald & Co (Publishers) Ltd
Maxwell House
74 Worship Street
London EC2A 2EN

A BPCC plc Company

For Sylvia

Part I

ACCIDENT

One

———◆———

The accident should never have happened. It had rained overnight but the sky was now clear, and at ten o'clock on that Monday morning the streets of Bonn were relatively quiet, the traffic light. But the Opel was travelling much too fast. The Herr Professor was late for his seminar, and he knew his students would be impatient. It was his wife's fault. She'd kept him arguing over the breakfast table when he should have been assembling his papers. Even now he wasn't sure that everything he needed for his day's work was in the black briefcase on the seat beside him. Angry, his mind preoccupied with his personal problems, he swung the car round the corner of the Hofgarten behind the University, and caught his breath at the figure of a woman directly ahead of him.

The Herr Professor was not a good driver. His reactions were slow and, in the face of the emergency, he panicked. He swerved indecisively from one side to the other, and his foot slipped from the brake to the accelerator. Even then the tragedy might have been avoided, but the woman panicked too. She hesitated, and in the space of a few seconds retreated, advanced a couple of steps, and again retreated. The Opel caught her on the hip and threw her brutally into the air before, slithering on the still damp road surface, it turned a full circle and slammed hard into a lamp standard on the other side of the street.

Only yesterday Martha Schmidt had celebrated her sixty-first birthday. It had been a modest party, a simple meal and a bottle of Frankenwein shared with friends. Martha was a widow, and her means were limited. But in the affluent

Federal Republic she managed to live quite comfortably on her pension – her husband had been a middle-grade civil servant in the West German Government – and there was a small nest-egg in the bank. She enjoyed her peaceful, un-eventful life, and today there was an added happiness – a letter from Otto.

Otto was her brother – her only brother, and she had no sisters. For twenty years she had believed him dead, but suddenly five years ago his letters had started to arrive. Normally one came in time for each of her birthdays, but this year's had been a day late. The letter's absence had worried Martha; after all, Otto was seven years older than she was, approaching sixty-eight, and one never knew. But at last, that very morning, it had been delivered, and all was well.

She remembered the first of Otto's letters; she almost knew it by heart. It had arrived shortly after her husband's death, just before she moved to her present apartment. Shocked, she had at first doubted its authenticity. But it had mentioned incidents during their childhood in Berlin, inci-dents known to no one but Otto and herself. It was genuine, all right. In spite of everything she'd heard and read, Otto had not been killed. She'd been filled with such joy that she'd wept.

Nevertheless, the letter had been strange. It had set down strict rules for their correspondence, if such a one-sided series of communications could be called correspondence. On no account must Martha hint that her brother was still alive. If any questions arose she must say the letters came from an old friend – Otto had even suggested the name of a girl with whom she'd been at school. He had given no address, and said that she must make no attempt to trace the source of this or any subsequent letters. She had in fact gone so far as to examine the postmark – Brussels – but had found that later letters had been posted in different cities in West-ern Europe and America. Finally, Otto had insisted that she read his letters immediately and then destroy them, saying nothing of their contents to anyone.

Clearly for some reason Otto needed to be circumspect, but just to be in remote touch with him gave Martha great pleasure. And, though the deceptions hadn't come easily to her over the years, especially when she didn't understand the need for them, she trusted her brother, and she had followed his instructions implicitly.

Until today. Today Martha Schmidt lay on her back in the gutter, barely conscious. Her thoughts, thready and fitful, were on Otto – and his letter. She hadn't read the letter yet, for the postman had come just as she was leaving the apartment block. She should have taken it back upstairs at once, but the lift was out of order, and she couldn't face the three-storey climb until she returned with her shopping. The letter would keep. Meanwhile she would enjoy knowing it was safe in her handbag.

Safe? The shock of the question poured adrenalin into Martha's system. She opened her eyes and stared hazily at the spring sky. Suddenly it was blotted out by a large face. Someone was bending over her, covering her with a coat. Martha paid no attention to the face. Instead she tried to raise herself to look around and search. She scrabbled on the road beside her for a moment, but pain shot through her body. She screamed in protest and sank back, the scream cut off as blood bubbled up into her throat, threatening to choke her. She gagged on the taste. She felt cold and very afraid. Then the pain ebbed slightly, and the large face materialized again, into that of a woman about her own age kneeling beside her. Martha felt her mouth being wiped.

'It's all right, *Liebling*. Just lie still. The ambulance is on its way. Everything will be all right.'

The voice was reassuring, but Martha knew that what it said wasn't true. She wasn't concerned for herself. The safety of the letter, Otto's letter, was paramount. The woman with the face was holding her hands in an attempt to restrain her, but Martha desperately tried to turn her head. As far as she could see, the bag wasn't there. It must have fallen elsewhere. It was no fault of hers, but the letter had been lost unread. The unknown consequences were vaguely terrifying. A tear trickled forlornly down Martha's cheek. A devout woman, through the miasma of her suffering she tried to pray.

'Frau Schmidt! Frau Schmidt!'

Martha Schmidt forced her eyes open, suddenly hopeful. Someone had spoken to her, addressed her by name. It must be someone who knew her, someone who would understand . . .

There seemed to be a lot of people gathered round her now, and a lot of activity. The woman who had been holding her hands had risen, and was looking down in pity. Beside the woman was a man in the green uniform of the West German police, with two men in white coats. On her other side, she recognized with relief a neighbour – Klaus Gerhardt. It was he who had spoken her name.

'Herr Gerhardt.'

Martha Schmidt mouthed the words rather than uttered them. He squatted down beside her. 'My – bag,' she whispered with difficulty. 'My handbag. The – letter.'

At once she saw the startled interest in his face, and she regretted the impulse that had made her appeal to him, and especially her mention of a letter. Klaus Gerhardt had been a colleague of her late husband's. She had known him a long time, but she had never liked him greatly. She'd always thought him over-curious, and hadn't been particularly pleased to discover, after she moved into her present apartment, that he lived very close. Nevertheless, he had always been pleasant to her, and in the past had done her several small kindnesses. Surely she could trust him now, when –

Martha Schmidt hardly felt the young doctor's quick examination or the prick of the hypodermic needle in her thigh. The morphine injection acted rapidly and she fell through blackness into unconsciousness, her worries forgotten. Gently she was lifted on to a stretcher and slid into the waiting ambulance. Meanwhile, the policeman had taken down what meagre particulars about her Herr Gerhardt could provide, and had turned to the woman who was an eye-witness of the accident.

Klaus Gerhardt picked up Martha's handbag from the pavement where someone had carefully placed it, unfortunately a little behind her head and thus out of her sight.

'I may go in the ambulance?' Gerhardt interrupted the policeman, his hand restraining the rear doors as they closed. 'As I said, I'm a friend of hers, and I'd like to accompany her. There is room for me?' He gestured across the road to where a green and white police car blocked his view of the crumpled Opel. 'What of the driver? Surely he's injured too?'

The policeman glanced up from his notes. 'Dead,' he said laconically. 'And pinned in the wreck. No need to wait for him.'

Bowing his head in acknowledgement, Klaus Gerhardt climbed into the back of the ambulance and sat himself beside the doctor. The attendant shut the doors behind them, hastened around to the front and got into the driving seat. The ambulance moved off.

'There is hope?' Gerhardt said tentatively, as if he were an anxious relative.

'There's always hope,' the doctor said, and added half under his breath, 'but this time it'll take a bloody miracle.'

Klaus Gerhardt smiled thinly. His hearing was excellent, and he'd caught the barely articulated mutter. He said no more. The raucous blare of the klaxon precluded conversation, and anyway he had no wish to talk. He sat, watching the uneven rise and fall of Martha Schmidt's chest, and wondered what was in the letter that seemed so important to her. Her handbag was on the seat beside him, but at the moment there was no chance of opening it. He let his fingers gently caress the clasp. He need only await his opportunity.

Herr Gerhardt was a small, gnome-like man with wispy hair and a pair of shrewd blue eyes. He had recently retired after an undistinguished career in the civil service, during part of which he had been deputy to the late Herr Schmidt. He had always made it a practice to find out as much as he could about his various superiors, but in the case of Schmidt most of the information he'd acquired had been singularly uninteresting. One fact, however, had impressed him. Before her marriage, Frau Schmidt had been a Fräulein Krasner, and the name Krasner was very familiar to him – as indeed it was to a great many Germans of his generation. As a result he had gone to considerable trouble and some expense to trace Martha Schmidt's background, and it had irked him that he had never found any use for what he'd learnt. Perhaps now, at last, his persistence was to be rewarded.

The klaxon that had been beating against his thoughts stopped suddenly, and Klaus Gerhardt became alert. The ambulance was slowing, coming to a halt. They had arrived at the hospital. The young doctor rose to his feet as the rear doors were flung open, and began to supervise the careful transfer of Martha Schmidt from ambulance stretcher to hospital trolley.

This was his chance, Klaus Gerhardt realized. While all attention was focused on the unconscious woman, he could act. Slowly he got to his feet. Then, his back half-turned as if he were making sure he had left nothing behind him, he flicked open Martha Schmidt's handbag and plunged in his hand. Keys, handkerchief, change purse, wallet, spectacle case, paper – but only a shopping list. Frustrated, he fumbled in the bottom of the bag. Something pierced his finger – a comb, a nail file – and he swallowed an oath. There was no letter.

'Herr Gerhardt!'

'Coming.'

Klaus Gerhardt's voice was steady, but he was trembling with a kind of rage. The stupid woman had deceived him with her blather about some precious letter in her bag. Why? She was as good as dead. Why should she lie? There must be a letter somewhere.

Nearly, so very nearly, he abandoned his whole ill-formed

purpose. But her bag was in his hand, so he took it with him. He climbed out of the ambulance and followed the others into the hospital's Casualty Department.

'Your name, please. And your address and phone number.'

Klaus Gerhardt answered unhesitatingly. He had nothing to hide. He was not, he explained, a relation of Frau Schmidt, but merely a friend, a neighbour, who had happened to be passing when the accident occurred.

'A good Samaritan,' the pretty nurse said, smiling at him.

Klaus Gerhardt shook his head in self-deprecation. 'No, no,' he said. 'Anyone would have done the same for a widow whose husband was once a dear colleague.'

The nurses nodded understandingly and, after a few questions about Martha Schmidt that Gerhardt answered to the best of his ability, asked if he would wait. 'Perhaps a cup of coffee?' she suggested.

'Thank you. You're very kind.' Klaus Gerhardt hesitated. An idea had come to him, and he wanted to test it as soon as possible. 'If I might first find a cloakroom . . .'

'Yes, of course. Around there to your right.'

The nurse pointed and, thanking her, Gerhardt walked down the green-painted corridor she'd indicated. He could feel her eyes on his back and had to force himself not to hurry. Every moment he expected her to call and ask if that were Frau Schmidt's bag he was carrying. But, swallowing hard, he rounded the corner, almost safe now, and hurried to the door bearing the international symbol for 'Men'.

There were two men in dressing-gowns in the lavatory, one standing at the urinal, the other washing his hands, but they were talking together and paid Klaus Gerhardt no attention.

He went to the cubicle furthest from them, and made a fuss of wiping the toilet seat with paper and flushing the bowl. Then he sat down and, for the second time, opened Martha's handbag.

Immediately his mouth widened into a smile, a smile of

satisfaction and anticipation. There was – as it had suddenly occurred to him there might be – a pocket in the side of the bag, which in his previous haste he had failed to notice. Unzipping it with fumbling fingers, he found what he was seeking – the letter.

To his surprise the envelope was unopened. Before slitting it with the nail file so thoughtfully provided by Frau Schmidt, he studied it carefully. It told him little. The envelope itself was cheap stationery that could have been bought almost anywhere in the world. The address – Martha Schmidt's address – was typewritten and accurate. The postmark was London four days ago.

The envelope contained two sheets of airmail paper, covered with small spidery handwriting. Instead of an address, the words 'From my home' appeared at the top of the first page. The date on the letter was nearly two weeks ago – a surprisingly long time, Klaus Gerhardt thought, between writing and posting.

Gerhardt turned to the end of the letter. There was no signature, as such, just the phrase 'Your loving brother'. He stared in disbelief. To his knowledge Martha Schmidt had had only one brother, Otto Krasner, and Krasner was dead. He read the letter slowly and carefully. It seemed to consist mainly of family news, which meant little to him. Nevertheless, it was a deeply satisfied man who folded the sheets of paper, replaced them in the envelope and slipped the envelope into his breast pocket. Gerhardt had no doubt that, offered to the right people, the letter would prove immensely valuable.

The cloakroom door opened, and there were voices outside the cubicle, clearly those of a patient and a male nurse. Hurriedly Klaus Gerhardt glanced again through the rest of the contents of the handbag, but there was nothing else to interest him. He flushed the toilet and let himself out of the cubicle. Nodding to the nurse who was helping a patient out of a wheelchair, he took his time washing his hands. Then he returned to the reception area.

The same pretty nurse brought him coffee and, as if he'd that moment remembered it, he gave her the handbag. She watched him drink. When he put down his cup she said, 'I regret I have bad news for you, Herr Gerhardt. Your friend has just died. Unfortunately there was nothing the doctors could do for her. Her injuries were too bad. There was really no hope.'

'Ah, poor Martha! Poor Martha! How very, very tragic.' Klaus Gerhardt shook his head sadly. 'Who would have thought this morning that . . .' He left the sentence unfinished, as if bereft of words. 'Well, I suppose there's nothing more I can do.'

The nurse looked at him anxiously. 'You should go home and rest, Herr Gerhardt. This has been a shock for you. Shall I get you a taxi?'

Klaus Gerhardt hesitated. Normally he would have refused – he was very careful with his money – but, remembering the letter, he changed his mind. 'Thank you,' he said with a small smile, 'that would be extremely kind.'

The address he gave the taxi-driver, however, was not that of his home, but a café well known to him, where he ordered beer with a shot of schnapps. Waiting for the drinks he patted his pocket to assure himself that the letter was still in place. He could scarcely believe his luck. At last his researches into Frau Schmidt's past could pay off. He'd come with her in the ambulance out of curiosity, on the offchance she might say more – and in case the policeman noticed him clutching her bag. But her death didn't matter. He'd got all he wanted. The main thing now was to keep his wits about him. He thought he knew the right contact. If he were careful, his morning's work would prove very rewarding.

Part II

BRIEFING

Two

———◆———

Five days later, having passed through various hands, the letter had reached London, and was being read by Colin Grenley, generally considered to be one of the most able Under-Secretaries at the Foreign and Commonwealth Office. When he reached the end, Grenley stared at the thin pages with feelings of incredulity and shock. He read them again, more slowly:

My dear Martha,

    Many happy returns of the day. I hope you have a good birthday. I only wish I could spend it with you but, as you know, that cannot be. The best I can do is to assure you of my love, and tell you that you are in my thoughts not only once a year, but all the time.

It was a great day for all of us, that day when you were born. After all, I was seven years old and I think our parents had given up hope of having another child. They were delighted with you. And so was I. I had always wanted a little sister, and you were so sweet. It's difficult to believe that so much time has passed since then, so much of our lives spent apart from each other. But I must not be morbid.

There is good news, and I don't only mean that I have almost finished the writing of my memoirs, though that is good news too. I am soon to be a grandfather, and that will make you a great-aunt. Isn't that wonderful? I could not be more pleased. Boy or girl? I don't mind in the least, though I think the proud parents would prefer their firstborn to be a son. They have promised to bring him – or her – to visit me as soon as possible. It's my one regret that they live so far away. Maybe my other girl will marry soon and there will be more grandchildren, with luck closer to home. I pray I'll still be here to see them.

Because there is something I must tell you, my little sister. My old heart isn't functioning as well as it should. The doctors say I'm fine, but I must take things easily, avoid stressful situations, and so on. You know, the usual spiel. So you're not to worry. But if anything should happen, I've arranged for you to know. There'll be a last letter.

With my prayers, as always.

Your loving brother.

The man sitting across the luncheon table from Colin Grenley gave him full marks for his composure, but the lengthening silence worried him. 'Is there some difficulty?' he asked. 'The language – the German?'

'No!' The reply was curt. Grenley prided himself on his gift for languages. Besides, after Oxford he had spent a year at the University of Heidelberg, and later in his career had been posted to Vienna. His German was near-perfect. 'Where did you get this?' he demanded. 'Who else has seen it? How can I be sure it's from Otto Krasner?'

The other man paused. 'That's a lot of questions,' he said. 'You know I never discuss my sources, but I can assure you that no one in the UK has seen it but me. As for its authenticity, if it were an *objet d'art* – as in a sense it is – I myself would guarantee its provenance.' He smiled, showing very regular, well-capped teeth.

Colin Grenley didn't return the smile. He entertained the art dealer at fairly frequent intervals, but always as a matter of duty and always at a restaurant, never at his club or his home. He didn't really like Svensen. Yet he'd bought one or two good pieces from him in the past, and the art dealer had proved himself useful in other ways, extremely useful.

An art dealer with a thriving international business often

24

picked up items of interesting information, especially when he was given a hint about what to look for. Clients were often garrulous, as if the act of making a purchase and writing a large cheque acted as a kind of release, and a tactfully worded question could sometimes elicit a surprisingly valuable reply. But this – this was in a different category altogether. It was certainly vastly more important than anything Svensen had provided before.

'If it's genuine, then the Americans must have pulled the wool over everyone's eyes,' Grenley said, surprised at the steadiness in his voice. 'The body they buried in 1958 can't have been Otto Krasner's. Krasner is still alive and well and living – somewhere.'

'You're stating the obvious,' said Svensen. 'And he's not all that well,' he pointed out. 'He's got some kind of heart condition.'

'Yes.' Grenley finished his brandy. His companion's glass was already empty, and he signalled the waiter to bring two more. He didn't usually drink much in the middle of the day, but now he felt he needed it.

'Look, Svensen,' he said. 'I know most of the bits of information you've given me in the past have proved authentic. But you know as well as I do that this – this matters. Why are you so sure of its provenance, as you call it?'

'I'll tell you this,' said the art dealer. 'That letter came straight out of the handbag of Krasner's sister, who was killed in a street accident in Bonn recently. From the text, it's clearly one of a series, and there's no reason to suppose the sister thought any of the past ones forgeries. If she had she'd probably have gone to the Federal Republic authorities long before this. Presumably she recognized the handwriting, or was convinced by references to their past lives or something. And –'

'And if Krasner's being kept under cover by the Americans,' interrupted Grenley, 'they're presumably controlling his correspondence, and they'd have made damn sure he told his sister to be discreet.' It fits together, he added to himself.

That Otto Krasner might be alive was incredible, but it looked as if they were going to have to act on the assumption that he was.

'The letter's dated two and a half weeks ago,' Grenley said. 'Have you got the original envelope?'

'Here. Typewritten. Addressed to Martha Schmidt in Bonn. Look at the postmark: it wasn't mailed till a week after it was written. Time for it to be censored, perhaps.'

'And it was posted in London W1. Which means that, wherever Krasner is, he's almost certainly not in the West End. At a guess I'd say he's not even in the UK. The USA's far more likely, though you never know. The Americans don't always do what's expected of them.'

Grenley stopped abruptly as the waiter appeared with the brandies. Christ, he thought, if only the Yanks hadn't been so antagonistic, hadn't played things so close to their chest. Not that anyone could blame them. It would have been a terrific boost for the CIA if, with Otto Krasner's help, they could have got the great Johann Meissener out of East Germany. But the Brits had messed it up for them – or so the Americans believed. And after that they'd seen no reason to co-operate or exchange any information about the operation. No reason at all. And now . . .

He said, 'Well, wherever Krasner may or may not be, it would be useful for us to talk to him,' and thought: With or without the blessing of the Yanks.

'I'm sure it would,' said Svensen. Once again the art dealer showed his teeth in a mirthless smile.

Colin Grenley looked deliberately at his watch. 'You'll have to forgive me,' he said. 'I'd forgotten how late it was. I must get back to the Office. There's a meeting scheduled for three-thirty and I can't miss it.'

'Of course.' Though he guessed the excuse was spurious, Svensen at once pushed back his chair.

Grenley stood too, and gripped Svensen's upper arm lightly. 'You won't mention this letter to anyone, will you? It's important.'

26

'In my business, I wouldn't have any clients if they couldn't trust my discretion,' Svensen said.

'And you'll let me know if you get anything else that might interest me?'

'As a matter of fact, I've a Russian icon that's just come into the gallery. Expensive, though.' Svensen mentioned a figure.

It wasn't an answer to his request, but Grenley had no doubt he'd been understood. 'Beyond my means,' he said.

'Wait till you see it. It's a bargain at today's prices. You know how many pseudo icons there are on the market at present. Not this one. It's a gem.' The dealer continued to talk artistic shop as Grenley saw him out of the restaurant and into a taxi. 'Come in next week and look at that icon,' he said finally, as Grenley shut the cab door for him.

'I might. Goodbye.'

Grenley turned away. He decided to walk back to the Office. He needed the exercise – he was putting on weight – and he needed to think, though not about icons. The letter, now safely in his wallet, had shocked him more than he cared to admit. It required a tremendous mental effort to adjust to the possibility – the probability – that Otto Krasner was not dead.

Striding down Whitehall towards the FCO, he swore under his breath. What a time to have this landed in his lap, he thought; from his point of view it could scarcely have been a worse moment. He was very busy with preparations for a major conference in Geneva in ten days' time. He was worried about an important posting for which he was in line. His mother, almost eighty, was becoming extremely demanding. His daughter was in the middle of an unhappy love-affair. And then there was the question of his own possible marriage to Julia, Lady Dencourt. All in all, he had enough problems without Otto Krasner rising from the dead.

Of course, the Krasner problem wasn't his alone. It was

possible he might not have to cope with it himself. But inevitably he would be involved and, before he consulted anyone or passed on the letter, he needed to check all the facts.

'I want every file relating to the abortive attempt by the East German philosopher and writer, Johann Meissener, to escape from the GDR in 1958. And I want them now,' he demanded immediately he reached his office.

His Personal Assistant was taken aback. Usually she found Colin Grenley a most considerate boss. But this little job would mean hours in the Records Department. And today was Friday. She'd been hoping to get away early, to meet a new boy-friend and spend a weekend in the country. She wondered if she dared make an appeal.

'You'll find cross-references to a GDR politician called Otto Krasner, who tried to cross the border with Meissener, and to Sir Francis Dencourt, our ambassador in Bonn at the time. I want all those files too.'

The PA bit off the words she'd been about to utter. Clearly any appeal was pointless. Grenley sounded grim, a sure sign of an impending crisis. But 1958! It was the year she herself had been born, the PA thought with a sudden flash of humour.

'As soon as I possibly can,' she said, doing her best to sound reasonably enthusiastic.

It was almost seven when the messenger carried the last heap of files into the Under-Secretary's office, and well after midnight before Grenley had finished with them. As he closed the last folder, he yawned and stretched. He was tired and depressed. His eyes felt gritty, his throat dry, his mind dull. It had all been a long time ago, but the files had brought the story back to him in detail: the attempted border crossing, Meissener's capture, Krasner's apparent death at the hands of the East German border guards. Then, the accusations of betrayal directed by the Americans against Francis Dencourt, accusations supported by the undoubted fact that Dencourt, an acknowledged womanizer, was having an affair with an East German girl, a refugee whom the CIA had been certain was an agent.

He had been in London at the time, and not directly concerned, but he remembered the case well – as past history. But suddenly it wasn't past any more, not in importance. If the letter were genuine – and Svensen had always been reliable – Otto Krasner was not dead, but an old man with a weak heart, writing his memoirs. And the whole affair could be raked up again, scrutinized, written about, gossiped about – and God knew where it would all end.

Colin Grenley sighed. He knew what would have to be done. They'd have to take immediate action to establish the true position. If Krasner was dead, so be it. If he weren't, they'd have to find him. It wasn't going to be easy. If the CIA had taken so much trouble to conceal the fact of the East German's survival and to hide him all these years, they wouldn't suddenly be prepared to reveal his whereabouts. No, no help could be expected from the Yanks. In fact, better not to ask. Renewed interest by the FCO in this long-forgotten operation would only serve to alert them. Quite a different approach was necessary. But what?

It was not until the beginning of the following week that Grenley was reminded of Hugh Merryck.

On Monday evening Colin Grenley went to a party given by Julia Dencourt, Sir Francis's widow. It was typical of Lady Dencourt's parties, in that almost all the guests were in their various ways important, or likely to become so. Tonight they included a former Prime Minister, a National Theatre star, a journalist noted for his bitter pen, a sprinkling of foreign diplomats and some very senior government officials. As for the women, they had more than their fair share of brains and influence, and a few were famous in their own right.

Grenley stood in the doorway and regarded them with a slightly jaundiced eye. He had come straight from the Office and, though he'd shaved and changed his shirt, he didn't feel as immaculate as he would have wished. Another party, and he might have cut it, sent flowers with his excuses the next day. But he couldn't do that with Julia. Julia was special.

'Colin, love, I thought you'd forgotten me.'

Abandoning the guests to whom she'd been speaking, Lady Dencourt came across the room to him. Even in her early fifties, she was still beautiful. Much of an age, she and Colin Grenley had been close friends for many years. They had met before her marriage to Sir Francis, when Grenley had been a junior official at the Foreign Office, just returned from his first overseas posting, and she had been very much a part of the London scene. Grenley remembered the surprise with which many of their friends – and the public – had greeted her engagement to a man, albeit a most attractive man, thirty years her senior.

Soon after the wedding, Sir Francis had taken Julia to Bonn when he took up his post as ambassador there, and Grenley had temporarily lost touch with her. Then had come the Establishment scandal associated with her husband. But she had survived it, and the gossip columns had coupled her name with many men since Sir Francis's death a few years later. Indeed, though she'd chosen to remain a widow, she might have remarried half a dozen times. As for her relationship with Colin Grenley, that had continued intermittently over the years, but they had become lovers only recently.

Julia held out both hands to him and he bent to kiss them, turning them so that his lips touched their palms.

'My most abject apologies, dearest Julia,' he said. 'You must blame the fact that service to Her Majesty must come before even you. In other words, I was kept late at the office.'

Julia smiled and took a glass from a passing waiter's tray, sipped it and held it out to him.

'Champagne?'

Grenley would have much preferred whisky, but he couldn't refuse. He lifted his glass to her. 'To the loveliest woman in London.'

Julia Dencourt laughed. 'Colin, you know most people here,' she said. 'Is there anyone you particularly want to talk to?'

'No – thank you.' Grenley glanced around the room and noted the Head of the SIS, General Sir Claud Bothwell, and one or two others with whom he might advantageously have a word. 'Don't worry about me.'

Julia nodded and let him go, and Grenley sauntered across the room to join the group around the former PM. He stood there for several minutes, listening attentively but volunteering little. Then, duty done, he moved on, greeting friends and colleagues at intervals.

'What's your view, Colin?'

Grenley had come to a stop beside another group, but he hadn't heard what was being discussed. 'Sorry,' he apologized. 'Afraid I'm not with you. I've had a hard day, and the mind tends to wander back to the FCO.'

There was sympathetic laughter. Then a grey-haired woman in a vivid emerald green dress said, 'We were talking about that Hampstead dinner-party two or three years ago, the one those terrorists attacked and took over. You must remember – it was all over the box and the papers for days.'

'Grenley, poor chap, was there. He was one of the hostages,' General Bothwell interrupted.

'Indeed I was,' Colin Grenley said, forcing himself to smile. Being held prisoner by heavily-armed terrorists for nearly a week was an experience he had no wish to recall.

But the woman continued. 'My sister, Lady Manserin – she was one of the guests too. She was so terrified she wouldn't go out for weeks afterwards. God knows what would have happened if the SAS hadn't stormed the place and rescued them. My sister says the people holding them were absolute fanatics. They'd easily have killed everyone without a qualm. Weren't you scared?' She turned to Grenley.

'Yes,' he said shortly.

31

'One woman was killed, wasn't she?' somebody else interposed.

'Yes, but that was an accident,' said the woman in the green dress. 'It was most unfortunate. During the final attack an SAS officer shot one of the woman hostages by mistake, and it turned out she was the wife of the ambassador of some country with which our relations were terribly delicate. There was a dreadful to-do about it. Poor wretched soldier! I wonder what became of him.'

Grenley and Bothwell exchanged sympathetic glances, and Grenley moved away, ostensibly to seek another drink. Christ, he thought, I can't take any more of that. It doesn't mean a damn thing to most of them, but to me . . . I'll never forget those days. And nor, God help him, will Hugh Merryck.

Grenley caught his breath as an idea struck him. A brilliant idea, surely, he thought. But he mustn't rush at it. He suppressed his excitement. Even if he decided on it, he'd have to get approval, and that might not be easy. Nevertheless, it was worth very serious consideration.

Three

During the two days that followed Lady Dencourt's party, Grenley established that the former SAS captain, Hugh Merryck, was still without regular employment, and obtained somewhat reluctant permission to use him in an attempt to trace Otto Krasner. Immediately, he telephoned the Merrycks' house on the Isle of Wight. Hugh Merryck might be available, but would he be willing?

'Hugh – Hugh Merryck?'

'Yes, who's that?'

'It's Colin Grenley here. Are you alone? Can you talk privately?'

'Hello, Colin. Yes, I'm quite alone in the house. My mother and father have gone into Ryde. Why? How are you?'

'I'm fine. And you?'

Briefly they exchanged pleasantries, then Grenley said, 'I'm glad I found you at home, Hugh. I gather that you're – free at the moment.'

'If you mean have I got any kind of regular job yet, the answer's no. I'm still unemployed and likely to remain so. You know perfectly well that the qualifications I've got don't make me particularly attractive to prospective employers.'

Grenley ignored the bitterness that Merryck had made no attempt to hide. He didn't blame the man. If anyone had ever had a raw deal, Hugh Merryck had.

'I might have something for you,' Grenley said bluntly. 'I doubt if it will lead to anything permanent, but while it lasts the money'll be good. Would you like to come up to London tomorrow to discuss it with me?'

Hugh Merryck said quickly, 'Colin, I'll be on the first boat and I'll take the job whatever it is without benefit of discussion, if you'll have me.'

'That's splendid!' Genuinely pleased, Grenley was relieved by Merryck's ready acceptance. 'Look, I'll be up to my eyes all the morning with meetings and God knows what else, but we can lunch together. You go straight to my club, Hugh – I'll tell them you're coming – and make yourself comfortable. I'll be along as soon as I can. Bring your passport and your international driving licence, if you've got one. And gear for two or three weeks. If you take the job, you'll be going abroad. And don't mention to anyone that the offer's come through me. It's all a bit – er – *sub rosa* at this stage, you understand. Okay?'

'I know what you mean. It's more than okay, Colin. Thanks a lot. I couldn't be more grateful.'

'Forget it, Hugh. I'm the one who should be grateful. You're just the man we want.' I hope and pray, Grenley added to himself. He'd made himself responsible for Merryck, and if Hugh let him down, made a mess of things, it was he – Grenley – who would suffer in the end.

But it was no use thinking of that now. Once it had been accepted that an outsider had to be used – someone deniable, who could if necessary be repudiated with conviction – Merryck was an obvious choice. Quite apart from his training and his talents, he had the kind of soldier of fortune image that could make a solo 'lone wolf' effort seem more credible if the operation went wrong and anything became public. In any case, no one had come up with a better possibility.

'Until tomorrow then,' Grenley said cheerfully. 'Goodbye.'

It was still dark the next morning when the alarm woke Hugh Merryck. He showered, shaved, dressed, not hurrying, and taking more than his usual care. When he was ready he inspected himself in the full-length mirror on the door of the old-fashioned wardrobe in his room.

He saw a man of thirty-two, though most people would

have guessed him to be older, tall and broad-shouldered, with light brown hair, blue eyes and a pleasant enough face. He was wearing a grey suit, a cream-coloured shirt and a foulard tie, not his customary jeans and sweater. There was a neat handkerchief in his top pocket, and his shoes shone.

'Not bad,' he said softly. 'Not bad at all.'

Suddenly he realized he was standing at attention and, letting his shoulders slump, he scowled at his reflection. He wasn't a soldier any more. He'd never be a soldier again. He'd dressed like this to satisfy his father and – he admitted, trying to be honest with himself – because he wanted to show Colin Grenley that two years of unemployment hadn't made a slob of him.

He heard his mother call and went downstairs. There was a wonderful smell of eggs and bacon. She had insisted on getting up to cook him breakfast and drive him to the boat. But he was surprised to see his father up and dressed.

'Thought I'd keep your mother company into Ryde,' the Brigadier said gruffly.

'Good idea.'

Hugh tried not to grimace as he saw his father's eyes flicker over him in a quick inspection, and noticed the involuntary nod of approval. At least today he'd come up to scratch, he thought sourly, no fatigues for sloppy dress. He felt the usual stab of resentment. Not that he could really blame his father.

Out of three sons, Brigadier Merryck might reasonably have expected that one would follow in his and his family's military footsteps. But the eldest had been lamed in a freak accident at school, and the middle boy had – perversely, according to the Brigadier – become a Roman Catholic priest. This had left Hugh, the youngest by five years.

At eighteen Hugh Merryck had gone willingly into the army and, after Sandhurst, had been commissioned into his father's old regiment. The Brigadier had almost burst with secret pride. But, though Hugh had done extremely well, his enthusiasm had waned. He had found peace-time soldiering

35

unexciting, the top brass too fond of spit-and-polish. When the opportunity arose, he had leapt at the chance to transfer to the Special Air Service, where he was soon involved in intelligence work. This he enjoyed.

Brigadier Merryck had been disappointed. He shared the regular officer's dislike of private armies, and his fears had been justified by the Hampstead siege. The publicity resulting from the killing of such an important hostage had been appalling. And with Hugh's inevitable resignation from the army had gone all his hopes.

Even when the worst was over and the scandal had subsided, life wasn't easy for either father or son. What was left of Hugh's meagre capital dwindled and he found himself forced to live at home, unable to get work, unhappy and bitter, while the Brigadier, who was quite incapable of showing his sympathy, grew more and more abrasive. Inevitably, in spite of Mrs Merryck's efforts, the situation between the two men deteriorated, so that by the time of Grenley's phone call it had become very tense.

'You haven't told us much about this job,' the Brigadier said, finishing his toast. 'Suppose you don't like it, Hugh?'

Hugh was mindful of Grenley's warning. Carefully he said, 'I'll know more when I get to London. But I intend to like it.' At the very least, he added to himself, I'll see it through, whatever my personal feelings, and make a success of it, however unpleasant or dangerous it turns out to be. Something might come of it, you never know.

Anyway, his own prospects apart, he owed Colin Grenley. It was Grenley, one of the rescued hostages on that ghastly night, who had later sworn with all the authority of his position that Captain Merryck's behaviour had been exemplary and that he was in no way to blame for what had happened. If it hadn't been for Grenley . . .

Hugh Merryck glanced at his watch. 'Time I went. I'll get my things,' he said shortly.

Some hours later Merryck was sitting in a deep leather armchair in the smoking-room of Colin Grenley's club, reading a morning paper, a gin and tonic on the table beside him. Grenley had been as good as his word, and from the moment Merryck arrived he'd been treated like a member.

Grenley came in as he was draining his glass. 'Hugh, it's good to see you. Sorry I'm so late.' They shook hands. 'Let's go straight in, otherwise they may not keep my table. I've booked one in a corner so that we can talk privately.'

'Whatever you say.'

As soon as they were seated, food in front of them, Grenley said, 'First, Hugh, I must impress on you that this job's extremely delicate – top secret, officially. We – the FCO – want to make certain enquiries, run a little operation if you like – on our own. We can't involve the SIS because it's – well, in a way it's an operation against an ally – the USA.'

Merryck looked up sharply.

'Naturally,' went on Grenley, 'we've got to conceal our part in the affair, which is why an outsider's ideal for the job. If anything goes wrong the FCO will have to deny you and so shall I, at least officially.'

'I see,' said Merryck slowly. 'But what about control and support and so on? Who's going to be responsible for all that – and for tradecraft – if you're dealing out Bothwell's crowd?'

'You know General Bothwell?'

'No, but I've a friend – Ian Hume – who works for him.'

Grenley nodded. 'Well, it's not quite that sort of job. Have you ever heard of Johann Meissener?'

'You mean the German writer chap who died in a so-called psychiatric institution in the GDR, though he was said to be saner than most of us?'

'Yes, that's him – he was a great man. Now, what about Otto Krasner? Does that mean anything to you?'

Hugh Merryck frowned. 'No, I'm sorry. I don't recall him.'

'That's not surprising. It was all before your time – in 1958, to be precise. Krasner was a politician, a friend of

Meissener's though much younger. They planned to escape from the GDR to the West together, but they were betrayed. Meissener was captured. Krasner got through, but was shot in the attempt. Supposedly he died just as he reached safety. At least, that's what the Yanks said. They even buried a body.'

'Not Krasner's body?'

'We don't think so. We've now got good reason to believe he may be still alive, though we don't know where. But you're going to establish the facts, find Krasner if he's alive and ask him some questions. At least, that's the job, Hugh. Will you take it?'

Merryic didn't hesitate. 'Yes,' he said. 'Of course I will. Tell me more.'

Grenley did just that, in a thorough briefing. He outlined the backgrounds of Johann Meissener and Otto Krasner. He told Merryck what was known of the way they came to make their tragic attempt to cross the border. He went on to Martha Schmidt and her letter, and why it seemed likely to be authentic. He produced a photocopy. 'Read it carefully and I'll take it back,' he said. 'It's the only bit of recent evidence, and we don't want it to get into the wrong hands.'

It was after three o'clock by now, and the two men were sitting behind coffee cups in a corner of the almost deserted club library.

'As to why we want to find Krasner,' continued Grenley, 'there are two points as far as you're concerned. The first relates to Sir Francis Dencourt, the British Ambassador in Bonn at the time.' He summarized Sir Francis's career, and the accusations of treachery and betrayal that had effectively put paid to it. 'What we hope is that Krasner will be able to clear Sir Francis, or at least suggest some way of proving that our ambassador wasn't responsible for betraying the escape attempt to the Soviet or GDR authorities. Secondly, we want to know what the hell might be in Krasner's wretched memoirs – any references to Dencourt, for example. God knows if he's really writing the damn things, or if the Agency would ever let them be published. But in the present state of UK – US relations they might, and the result could conceivably be catastrophic. At the very least we need to know in advance what's in them, so that we can prepare ourselves.'

Grenley paused and took a sip of cold coffee. 'Look, Hugh,' he added, 'I know it's all a long time ago and Sir Francis is dead and the whole thing may seem outdated and of minor importance. But you can take it from me it matters. Let's say it matters to us to clear up some of the shit that was flung at Britain and the FCO because of the Meissener–Krasner case, and to make sure no more's likely to come our way. That's all you need to know.'

'I understand,' Merryck said.

'Don't think it's going to be simple,' Grenley concluded. 'Let's assume Krasner's alive. If the CIA become aware of your efforts to trace him – and it's almost inconceivable they won't – they'll try to put every obstacle in your way. He was an important defector – pretty high up in GDR Government circles – and they must have guaranteed him absolute security in return for his co-operation. A compromise now would be a disaster for them. Quite apart from their responsibility to Krasner, it would be bad for their reputation in the trade if the story became public; future would-be defectors need to know they can trust their hosts and, because of the Dencourt connection, they could never be sure we wouldn't go public. Now, before we get down to practicalities, have you got any questions?'

Merryck hesitated for a moment, then he said, 'Yes. If Krasner knew anything of interest about Sir Francis's role in the escape attempt, surely he'd have told the CIA immediately.'

'We've thought of that point, too. The answer's yes, possibly – if he was questioned about it at the time, and if he realized the significance of anything he knew. You've got to remember he was badly wounded in the border crossing, and it's probable he was seriously ill for some months after he reached the West.' Grenley picked his words carefully. 'Anyway, the Americans were thoroughly convinced of Francis's guilt. Their main point was that he was having an affair with an East German girl, who they maintained was a GDR agent. They were hopping mad about it. In addition, they'd have wanted to interrogate Krasner on a great many crucial, topical questions, and they might not have bothered about Dencourt – certainly they wouldn't have been looking for evidence to clear him. They left Dencourt to us and, of course, we believed Krasner was dead.'

'I see,' said Merryck.

'Anything else?'

'Colin, I'd like to know. Do you believe Sir Francis was innocent?'

'Yes – and his wife, his widow, is convinced of it.' To Merryck's surprise, Grenley gave a slightly embarrassed grin. 'I suppose I'd better come clean. I've got a personal interest in the case. If she'll have me, I'm hoping to marry Julia Dencourt.'

'Well – congratulations!' Merryck hid his amusement. He had never before seen Colin Grenley other than completely self-possessed. 'It sounds an excellent idea.'

'It was an excellent idea until –' Grenley shrugged. 'Hugh, I'm an ambitious man. I've never pretended otherwise. As long as this business of Francis was past history and forgotten, it didn't matter. But if the whole thing's raked up again and there's a public scandal, I'd be faced with an unpleasant choice – between Julia and my career. I hope that doesn't make me sound too much of a heel, but that's the truth of the matter.'

Merryck smiled his sympathy. He had no intention of passing judgement on Grenley's private affairs. Instead, he reverted to an operational question. 'Colin, suppose the Yanks catch on to me – and you say they will – what explanation do I give for my activities – my enquiries about Krasner?'

'If you have to, say you're acting on behalf of the Dencourt family. That's quite reasonable – and it's true in a way. But don't be specific.'

Changing the subject abruptly, Grenley began to discuss administration. There would be no question of cover or a legend for Merryck; he'd use his own name and passport. He wouldn't figure on any FCO payroll, but regular sums would be credited to his bank. 'The secret vote, you know,' Grenley said, passing over a thick envelope. 'That should cover you for a while. After that, use any credit cards you've got, draw on your bank or contact me.'

'How?' said Merryck at once. 'What about communications?'

'I was just coming to that. Remember this number and call at regular intervals. We can't help you much, but we need to know where you are. As you see, it's not the usual FCO office number. It's official, but it's a direct line. If I'm not there, whoever answers will get a message to me. Report your movements, or arrange money matters or things like that. But remember, on any matter of substance, you deal with me and me alone. Wait for me to get back to you. Understood?'

'Yes,' said Merryck. It had been a curiously casual briefing, quite unlike the kind of orders he'd been given for undercover operations in his SAS days. But in the circumstances he supposed it was not unreasonable. There was one question that remained, and it wasn't until they were saying goodbye on the steps of the club that Merryck had a chance to ask it. 'Colin, what if I find Krasner, and he just tells me to go to hell?'

'My dear Hugh,' Grenley laughed, 'you're a persuasive chap. If that happens it'll be up to you.'

This was a singularly unsatisfactory answer, but Merryck didn't try to argue. It was quite clear to him that Grenley hadn't been entirely frank about the reasons either for the mission, or for the exclusion of the SIS. Undoubtedly there was a great deal more to it than they thought he needed to know. But his not to reason why. His immediate task was practical – to find the German. And he had to succeed for his own sake, to prove to himself he could still undertake a delicate and demanding job. As Grenley had said, it was unlikely to be a walkover. After twenty-five years, Otto Krasner might be a very distant stranger.

Part III

OPERATION

Four

---◆---

The following day the Lufthansa lunch-time flight serving Cologne and Bonn was delayed for over an hour at Heathrow, and didn't reach Wahn airport in the Federal Republic until after three o'clock in the afternoon. Merryck passed rapidly through the West German immigration controls; he had a minimal wait for his baggage, and the Customs did not bother him. An excellent lunch had been provided on the aircraft, and by now he was very little behind schedule.

Merryck's German, though a trifle rusty, was fluent. His father had once served as a senior staff officer at Rhine Army Headquarters, and Merryck had spent several school holidays at Müchengladbach. His parents had had the good sense to live 'on the economy' off the base, and young Merryck, proud of his gift for languages, had missed no opportunity to practise and display it. Now, he had no difficulty in arranging to rent a car, and soon found himself behind the wheel of an almost new Audi, driving confidently but circumspectly south-west from the Cologne/Bonn airport. Some twenty-five minutes later he arrived in the capital, and drew up in front of his hotel in the Poppelsdorfer Allee.

'You will be staying how long, sir?' the hotel receptionist asked.

Merryck had done some tentative planning. Inevitably the plans were fluid, but he had a mental list of the people he wanted to see. They might lead to others, either in Bonn or elsewhere. Alternatively, if he came to a dead end here, he would go to Berlin, where Martha Schmidt and her brother had lived as children, and try to pick up a thread there.

'Over the weekend, till Monday, at least,' he replied. 'Possibly longer. That will be all right?'

'Perfectly, sir. Now, would you like your car garaged?'

'No. I'll be needing it again almost immediately. I'll be down as quickly as I can.'

Shown to his room, Merryck washed, rubbed an electric razor over his face and put on a clean shirt. He was wearing the suit he'd worn yesterday for his lunch with Colin Grenley. With his old briefcase, now filled with a street map of Bonn, a Michelin guide to the area and some hotel writing paper, he looked the part he had decided upon – a professional man of some kind, concerned with the law. He inspected himself in a mirror for a moment and, satisfied, went downstairs.

In the lobby of the hotel was a giant wall-map of the city. Buttons beside the list of 'places not to be missed' caused indicator lights to appear. Merryck tried the Rathaus and Poppelsdorfer Schloss and the house where Beethoven was born, but his eyes were checking the location of the street where Martha Schmidt had lived. As he'd thought, it was only a short distance from the hotel. He turned away and went out to his car.

He drove twice past the unpretentious block of apartments on Marienstrasse before parking and ringing the janitor's bell. As he waited he looked about him. It was a pleasant neighbourhood, the street tree-lined and quiet, with an air of modest prosperity. For the first time he wondered seriously what sort of person Martha Schmidt had been. A lot might depend on whether she'd been a gregarious woman, talkative and with many friends, or a solitary type.

'*Guten Tag, mein Herr.*'

Hugh Merryck returned the greeting and produced what he hoped was a reassuring but confident smile. The woman in front of him was short and plump, with grey hair drawn back in a neat bun and a pleasant, friendly face, bereft of all make-up. She looked like anyone's grandmother. But she

46

stood four-square in the entrance, blocking any attempt that Merryck might make to enter.

Merryck said, 'I'm sorry to disturb you, *gnädige Frau*, I understand that Frau Martha Schmidt lives here, but I don't know the number of her apartment.'

'You are perhaps a cousin?' she said as if the idea amused her.

Merryck was startled by the question. 'No, I'm no relation. I represent a client in England. It's a legal matter.' He stopped abruptly as if he had caught himself saying too much, being indiscreet.

'Frau Schmidt is no longer here.'

'She's moved away? Do you have her new address?'

'She is dead, mein Herr.'

'Dead? Oh no. But how –?'

'It was a traffic accident, two weeks ago next Monday. She was crossing the road and this professor from the university – a man like that, he should have known better – he was driving much too fast. His car hit her and killed her. Such a good woman. It was a great tragedy.'

'I'm so sorry, Frau –?'

'Frau Schneider.'

'She was a friend of yours, Frau Schneider?'

'Yes, indeed. She was a widow, you know, like me, and often she'd come down to my apartment for a chat and a cup of coffee. Sometimes I'd go upstairs to her. Or we would go out to a café together.' Frau Schneider sniffed loudly. 'I shall miss her very much.'

'I am sure you will.' Merryck hesitated, frowning. A little doubtfully he said, 'Since Frau Schmidt is regrettably deceased, I shall need to find her nearest relatives, her heirs. If you could perhaps help, I should be very grateful.'

Frau Schneider gave him a shrewd, appraising glance, and he guessed that, for all her kindly air, she was nobody's fool. But obviously she liked to talk, and Martha Schmidt's violent death had provided her with an unusual opportunity.

well,' she said at last. 'I may be wrong, but you seem
t from the others. Come in.'
ank you, Frau Schneider. Incidentally, my name is
Merryck.'

Acknowledging this information with a nod of her head,
Frau Schneider stood back from the door and led the
way down a passage to her apartment. Merryck followed,
thankful to have been found more acceptable than 'the
others', whoever they might be. She waved him to a seat
on a plush-covered settee. He put his briefcase by his
feet.

'I have just made myself some coffee, Herr Merryck, if you
would care to join me?'

'Thank you. That would be wonderful.'

Left to himself for a moment, Merryck looked around the
room at the dark curtains and the heavy furniture, and the
family photographs on the piano. Everything was spotlessly
clean. Wood was lustrous, china figurines on the mantel
shone. Floorboards, visible around the neat rugs, were highly polished. The room was obviously little used.

Frau Schneider came in with a tray, on which were a
coffee-pot and cups, scones and cake. 'All home made,' she
said proudly, as Merryck got up to help her.

'You're very kind.'

'That we shall see, Herr Merryck.' Frau Schneider paused
for effect, then, smiling widely, said: 'You wanted to meet
Martha Schmidt's relations and heirs. Well, you see an heir
before you.'

'Indeed, do I? You must have been a really close friend,
then?'

'I was. I think I could truthfully say her only one, though
there was an old schoolfriend she heard from occasionally.
But she never saw her. It was because of me that she came to
live here after her husband's death. She left me her jewellery
– it's not a great deal, but there are a couple of very nice
pieces – and a water-colour of the Rhine that I always
admired. Everything else goes to the church, to be spent as

Father Anselm sees fit. Again, there's not a large amount. Her widow's pension died with her, of course.'

'And no relations?' Merryck prompted, accepting a second scone he didn't want but eager not to upset Frau Schneider's flow of words. 'Didn't you say something about cousins?'

'All Martha's relations are in the East, in the Democratic Republic – and she had no contact with them. You won't remember the war and the division of Germany afterwards. You're too young, Herr Merryck. But many families were separated then.' Frau Schneider sighed gustily. 'Fortunately for Martha she was married, and she and her husband were settled in the West, in what has now become the Federal Republic – but they found themselves cut off, isolated. Herr Schmidt did have a few relatives in the West – a nephew and his wife came to Martha's funeral – but she hadn't been in touch with them for years, not since her husband died. The Schmidts had no children of their own, of course.'

'She must have been a very solitary lady.'

'Yes, but she wasn't unhappy. She was self-contained and she lived a quiet life, but she was well contented.' Frau Schneider was silent for a moment; she was enjoying herself. 'Which is why, mein Herr, I find it so strange that her death should occasion such extraordinary interest.'

Merryck hid his curiosity. He finished the piece of cake he was eating and held out his cup. 'Could I, please? It's such excellent coffee.'

Frau Schneider poured the coffee, then continued as if he hadn't interrupted. 'It's natural the police should ask questions, since Martha met a violent death. And Herr Kaufmann too, her lawyer, who made her will and has to settle her affairs, simple though they may be. There are things he needs to know. But two so-called cousins, and now you, Herr Merryck.' She shook her head in disbelief, her shrewd eyes bright. ·

'Frau Schneider, I know nothing about any cousins,' Merryck said firmly, wondering if an FCO man, perhaps

49

someone from the Bonn embassy, had already made an undercover attempt to interrogate her.

'The first one was a German. He said he came from Mainz, but Martha had never mentioned him. He wanted to look through her apartment – he said she had papers that belonged to the family – but I wouldn't let him. I told him that such papers as there were, and Martha wasn't one for keeping things, had been taken by the lawyer. But he never went to see Herr Kaufmann. I checked.'

'Very sensible of you, Frau Schneider. What about the second man? Did you send him to the lawyer too?'

'I did. But he preferred to question Herr Bunge, our postman, instead. It seems he was curious about Martha's mail. Did she receive many letters from abroad? When was the last? Such questions! Herr Bunge told me about them himself.'

'Very strange,' Merryck said, and meant it. 'This second man, was he German too?'

'No. He spoke German fluently – rather like you, only a little better – but I'm sure it wasn't his native tongue.'

Merryck pondered for a few minutes. Neither of the 'cousins' had the stamp of an FCO man. The first, the German – and Frau Schneider could surely be trusted not to make a mistake about this – he couldn't place at all. The second, the non-German, could possibly be CIA. If the Americans had kept an eye on Krasner's sister, as was quite likely, they'd have known of her death, and been anxious to ensure that the last letter he'd sent her didn't go astray or get into the wrong hands. Merryck disliked the idea that ahead of him were two unknowns, at whose purposes he could only guess.

He got to his feet. 'Frau Schneider, I must go. You've been very helpful to me. Thank you.'

'But is that all you want?' Clearly she was disappointed.

'Why, yes.' He grinned at her. 'I don't know what those two men were after but, as for me, I'm satisfied. I can phone my client in London and report what you've told me, that poor Frau Schmidt is dead and has left no close relations. After that I'll hope to catch the next flight home.'

Reiterating his thanks, and noting the address of Herr Kaufmann's law firm that Frau Schneider insisted on giving him, he said goodbye. He had learnt a lot about Martha Schmidt, and was grateful. Unfortunately, he thought, as he drove slowly through the grey streets of Bonn, none of it seemed likely to further his search for Otto Krasner.

Nevertheless, as soon as he reached his hotel he tried Herr Kaufmann's phone number. He was sure that lawyers in the FRG were no different from lawyers anywhere else; they weren't in the habit of working late on Friday afternoons. But there was a chance that someone might still be in the office, and could give him Kaufmann's home address.

His luck was in. The lawyer, delayed by a conference with a valuable client, answered the phone himself, and Merryck at once launched into his story. It was the story he had told Frau Schneider, but more specific. He claimed to represent a well-known London firm of solicitors. The chances that Kaufmann would bother to check on him were remote, and the risk worth taking. Even if the London firm did deny all knowledge of him it would scarcely matter.

'Yes. Yes. I know them.' Herr Kaufmann said impatiently. 'We had dealings with them a couple of years ago over an estate. But, mein Herr, you must appreciate this is no way to do business – over the telephone. Come in on Monday, and I'll do my best to be of assistance. Let me get my appointments book.'

'Please, Herr Kaufmann, don't bother. I shall be back in London on Monday. It was only because I was in Köln that I thought of calling on Frau Schmidt. We had no idea she had met with an accident.'

'You had corresponded with her?' There was the faintest trace of suspicion in the lawyer's voice.

Merryck thought quickly. 'No. The matter has just arisen. A small inheritance, which will now go to Frau Schmidt's next of kin. That is where I'd hoped for your help, Herr

Kaufmann. If you could give me the name and location of her nearest blood relative, I'd be most grateful. It is a little informal, I know, but it would save all of us wasting time over what is really a trifling affair.'

Unfortunately Herr Kaufmann couldn't help. He had met Frau Schmidt only three or four times, in connection with her husband's estate, and her own will after her husband's death. As far as he could recall, she had never spoken of any relations. Nor were any mentioned in her will or in the few papers she had left. He assumed she had been alone in the world since her husband died.

Merryck thanked him profusely and put down the receiver. He was not disappointed. Herr Kaufmann had said no more than he had expected, and confirmed his belief that Martha Schmidt had been a very discreet woman.

Yet someone had known enough about her to realize the significance – and value – of that letter. How had he or she got hold of it in the first place? Grenley had said the letter had been taken from Martha's handbag, the implication being that this had happened at the time of the accident. Any passer-by could have picked up the bag. Police? Ambulance-men? Hospital staff? The answer was to start with the hospital and work backwards. But not now, not tonight. Right now what was wanted was a couple of drinks and a good dinner.

Five

It rained overnight and Bonn was looking much as it had on the morning that Martha Schmidt was killed, the streets glittering with moisture, the trees dripping sadly, but the sky lightening and the mist by the Rhine almost completely dissipated. Hugh Merryck reached the hospital at ten o'clock, parked his Audi and found the Casualty Department. Apart from a small boy with an anxious mother and a tear-stained face, there was no one about.

A nurse appeared quite soon, told Merryck that she would only be a moment, and led the small boy and his mother away. A policeman brought in a youth who seemed dazed but otherwise unharmed.

'Fell off his motor-bike,' the policeman said to the nurse when she reappeared a few minutes later. 'Skidded on some wet leaves. But he was lucky. Just hurt his leg, I think, and a bit shocked.'

The nurse looked at Merryck. 'Take the young man first,' he said, in answer to the unspoken question.

'That was good of you,' the nurse said to Merryck when she returned to the reception area after dealing with the youth. 'Now, what's the trouble?'

'No trouble, so I wasn't really being kind.' Merryck grinned at her. 'If you're not too busy, I'd like to ask a few questions – about a Frau Schmidt, Martha Schmidt, an elderly lady who was hurt in a street accident. She was knocked down by a car, and she died subsequently. Some ten days ago it must have been.'

'I remember. I was on duty when she was brought in.' The nurse, who had been friendly and forthcoming, was suddenly very businesslike, almost hostile. 'What do you want to know? We've already had other enquiries about Frau Schmidt.'

'Have you indeed?'

The nurse didn't respond. Unluckily for Merryck she wasn't garrulous like Frau Schneider. She waited and he was forced to continue.

'It's concerned with an insurance claim.' He ignored her disbelieving smile; she'd heard that story before. 'Am I right in assuming that everything Frau Schmidt had with her when she arrived at the hospital was listed?'

'Quite right. Clothes, rings, jewellery, watch, everything – down to the last pfennig in her handbag.' The nurse was triumphant. 'So if anything's missing, it was lost or stolen while she was lying in the street, before the police and the ambulance arrived. Unless you're thinking of accusing the police or the ambulancemen – or the kind neighbour who came to the hospital with her.'

'I'm not going to accuse anyone,' Merryck said mildly. 'It's merely a formality, checking that nothing could have gone missing. If she had a friend with her, the problem's solved.'

'He wasn't with her when she was knocked down. He just happened to see the accident and once he realized who it was, who'd been hurt, he couldn't just leave her, he said.'

Merryck shrugged. 'It comes to the same thing. He can witness that all was as it should be. He sounds a nice man. I'm sure he wouldn't mind.'

'No, I don't suppose he would, but –'

'So, if you could give me his name and address, it'd be a big help. It would save me having to go to the police.'

'Yes – all right.'

She was still a little reluctant, but clearly the mention of the police had swayed her in his favour. Merryck was amused at her lack of logic. But he was thankful that he was about to get what he wanted without further trouble or argument. He wondered if she had been as co-operative over the 'other enquiries' she'd received, and recognized this as useless speculation. Doubtless he'd find out for himself in time.

The nurse was now sorting through some papers. 'It's not here, and I can't remember,' she said. 'I think his name was Gerhardt, but I'll have to make sure.'

Merryck sat down to wait. The telephone rang and a different nurse appeared to answer it. She ignored Merryck, who pretended to be reading a magazine. A man dashed in, bearing a child in his arms; apparently the child had drunk some kind of cleaning fluid. Suddenly the casualty reception area came to life. A woman was brought in on a stretcher; from the conversation Merryck gathered that she had fallen downstairs. A wife accompanied her husband, grey-faced and clasping his chest; a coronary? Nurses and doctors came and went as the patients were processed and removed for treatment. Merryck continued to wait.

Time passed. Merryck had begun to think that he could sit there indefinitely, when the nurse to whom he had spoken was standing in front of him. She thrust a piece of paper into his hand.

'Sorry I've taken so long. I got caught up.'

'I understand. Many thanks.'

Glad to be outside again, away from the slight smell of antiseptic inside the hospital, Merryck drew in deep breaths of cold, damp Rhineland air as he walked to his car. The nurse had been right, he saw, glancing at the name and address she'd written down for him. Martha Schmidt's kind neighbour was called Gerhardt – Klaus Gerhardt. Merryck felt excitement rise in him. Could Herr Gerhardt be his first real lead to Otto Krasner?

Like Martha Schmidt Herr Gerhardt lived in a small apartment building, though one less well-kept, the paint of the woodwork beginning to peel, the front steps in need of a good scrub. Even the street, though close by Marienstrasse, was a little noisier, a little shabbier. The outer door of the building

55

was open, so Merryck was able to run up the stairs and press the bell of Apartment No. 6.

There was no answer, and an envelope sticking out from the underside of the door suggested that Herr Gerhardt was not at home. Merryck tried again, keeping his thumb hard down on the bell-push. Gerhardt, he thought, was probably at work. He was turning away from the door when a boy came bounding down the stairs.

He stopped when he saw Merryck at Herr Gerhardt's door and said, 'If you're wanting Klaus I think he must be away. We've not seen him for days.'

'Thanks.'

Slowly Merryck followed the boy out of the building. There seemed to be no resident janitor, no one he could ask when Herr Gerhardt might be home again. Yet the more he thought about it, the more convinced he was that Gerhardt was a likely person to have stolen Martha Schmidt's letter.

At that moment he saw the boy running back, clutching a large loaf. 'Hi,' he said. 'Do you know where Herr Gerhardt works?'

'He doesn't work, not any more. He's an old man, retired.' The boy pulled a bit of crust off the loaf and ate it. 'He used to work for the Government, a sort of clerk. Now he lives on his pension.'

'Is he likely to be away for long?'

'No. He'll probably be home tomorrow, or Monday.'

Merryck thanked the boy, though he didn't necessarily believe him. He had an idea the boy had merely told him what he thought would be acceptable. Probably there was no knowing when Gerhardt would return. But he had to be seen and questioned. There was no alternative, Merryck decided, to hanging around in Bonn, at least for a few days.

Lost in his thoughts, Merryck suddenly realized he was driving past a large Gothic church. He braked sharply. Frau Schneider had said that Martha Schmidt had left most of her small estate to a Father Anselm, to be used as he saw fit. This could well be the church, and Father Anselm might well be worth a call.

But once again Merryck was out of luck. It was Father Anselm's afternoon for visiting the prison. When he returned he would be hearing confessions and later he would be occupied with his next day's sermon. If another priest could be of service the housekeeper would be happy to fetch one. Merryck shook his head.

'No. It's a personal matter. I need to speak to Father Anselm himself. What about tomorrow?'

'Tomorrow? But tomorrow is Sunday, mein Herr.' The housekeeper was horrified. 'He'll be busy until the late evening. Unless it's an emergency, absolutely impossible.'

Merryck couldn't honestly claim it was an emergency in the sense intended by the housekeeper, but he said tentatively, 'I may be leaving Bonn on Monday and –'

To his surprise the housekeeper volunteered, 'On Monday Father says the early mass. You could see him after breakfast. About eight-thirty? That would suit you, perhaps?'

'Yes, it would. Many thanks.'

Grateful, Merryck left the presbytery and collected his car. For the moment he seemed to have come to a dead end. He proposed to spend the rest of the afternoon walking and refreshing his memories of Bonn.

It was while he was strolling gently among the old trees of the Hofgarten behind the University that he suddenly had the impression he was being followed. He glanced around, taking care to seem casual. Some twenty yards behind him were a woman pushing a pram and a large man. As Merryck's gaze passed over them, the man spoke to the woman, and Merryck abandoned him to consider a couple of teenagers, their arms around each other, two elderly women and another man with a dog. None of them looked in the least suspicious and Merryck, angry with himself and his jitters, continued to walk.

A minute or two later the dog, a standard poodle, came

galloping up beside him, and it was natural for Merryck to look over his shoulder for the owner. The woman with the pram was sitting on a bench, but the man who had been speaking to her had moved away. They were obviously not together. Merryck walked on, guessing that it hadn't been his imagination. He had a watcher.

Merryck left the Hofgarten and made his way through the streets past the Rathaus to the market-place. Lingering among the gaily-coloured stalls, he found it easy to spot his tail. It was the big man he'd noticed before, and Merryck reproached himself for not having identified him sooner. But he hadn't expected to be under observation. Indeed, he had reason to believe that the others interested in Martha Schmidt were ahead of him, and he'd made no attempt to conceal his movements. But it was clear that someone, or some authority, had been keeping an eye on Martha Schmidt's friends and contacts, and he'd been picked up in the course of the surveillance.

Choosing his moment carefully, Merryck dived between two of the stalls and, keeping out of the man's line of vision, hurriedly retraced his steps. His object was to come up behind his tail. He'd noted the man's quiet check jacket and had no difficulty in spotting him again. He approached him fast, seized his arm above the elbow and said, 'Here I am, mein Herr.'

The man whipped round. 'Who are you? What do you want?'

Merryck retained his grip, and inspected his catch. Medium height, with medium brown hair and nondescript clothes, he looked like a none-too-affluent businessman, but he was broad and very strongly built. Merryck paused before replying.

The man took instant advantage of Merryck's hesitation. 'Let go my arm,' he said, 'or I'll call the police. There are two of them over there. Look.'

Merryck paid no attention to such an obvious ploy. Even if there were police near by he did not believe the man would want to involve them. It was a bluff to distract him. His fingers dug deeper, seeking the nerve.

'Why are you tailing me?' he demanded. 'Who are you working for?'

'Tailing you? I'm not tailing you. I'm here on holiday.' The man squirmed. Then suddenly he shouted. 'Help! Help! Police!'

It wasn't a bluff, Merryck realized, as two burly green-uniformed figures came running. He released the man's arm and waited for him to speak, to offer the explanations the police would expect. Rubbing his arm, the man glared at him.

'Trouble?' the older policeman asked.

'This guy accosted me. I think he wanted money. I didn't quite understand, but he was getting unpleasant. You were there and I thought it sensible to ask for your help.'

'I see.' The policeman turned to Merryck. 'And what have you to say?'

'It was a misunderstanding. I thought I recognized him as someone I'd met.' Purposely Merryck spoke haltingly to show he was a foreigner.

'Identification, *bitte*.'

Merryck reached in his breast pocket and produced his passport. He had been slower than the other man, and had to hand it to the younger policeman.

'You are British? *Ja*. What are you doing in Bonn, mein Herr? Are you here on business?'

'No – *nein*. A few days holiday. That is all.'

'Where are you staying?'

The last question came from the older – obviously the more senior – policeman, and was abrupt. His attitude to Merryck seemed to have changed. At first he had been neutral, even disinterested. Now he was hard, suspicious, aggressive.

'At the Bristol.'

'The Bristol? We can easily check that, you know.'

Merryck shrugged. 'That's where I'm staying.'

59

'For how long?'

'Until Monday.'

'You are leaving Bonn on Monday? Where are you going?'

The questions came fast, and all directed at Merryck. The other man stood by, apparently immune. Yet, apart from his first accusation, he'd said nothing, done nothing – except show his passport. Merryck curbed his tongue, stumbled over his German and played the innocent.

Eventually the man intervened. It was possible he'd misunderstood the *Engländer*. Anyway he had no wish to press charges. Thanks to the fortunate presence of the police no harm had been done. He would prefer to forget the whole thing. With a laugh he added, 'It's not worth an international incident.'

Grinning, the two policemen agreed and, with a casual wave, the man walked off. Merryck watched his retreating back speculatively.

'Okay then, mein Herr,' the policeman said, once more relaxed and in a good humour. 'It is agreed. A misunderstanding. But if you're going to recognize anyone else you don't know, try not to choose a GDR diplomat.'

'No, I won't,' said Merryck. '*Danke schön.*'

'*Bitte, mein Herr,*' said the policeman.

Merryck wasn't being sarcastic. He was indeed very grateful to the policeman. As he left the market square in the direction of his hotel, he thought that the cop had told him almost all he might have hoped to shake out of the man who had undoubtedly been tailing him. And it wasn't good news. He didn't really like the idea that the East German security or espionage services were so interested in him and, presumably, his mission.

Six

Sunday was a day of frustration as far as Merryck was concerned. There was no one to see and nothing to do that could further his enquiries. In the afternoon he drove to Bad Godesberg and walked beside the Rhine, watching the barges glide by, and admiring the romantic peaks of the Siebengebirge on the other side of the river. As far as he could tell, no one followed him or took the slightest interest in him.

He had intended to wait until Monday before revisiting Gerhardt's apartment building but, after dinner, still restless and bored with inaction, he changed his mind. It was not a great distance and he decided to walk. He chose a slightly circuitous route, and once doubled back on his tracks. Again there was no watcher.

And again it was all a waste of effort. He was lucky in that the outer door of the building was still wide open, but Klaus Gerhardt was clearly still away. The same brown envelope was still jutting from beneath the door of his apartment, and his bell remained unanswered. If Merryck had not been so conscious of his totally wasted day he might have left it at that, but somehow in the circumstances this was the last straw.

In the hallway, before he activated the time-switch that turned on the staircase lights, Merryck had subconsciously noticed the front door of another apartment, with a bright glow shining around its edges. Now he saw that Herr Gerhardt's door was equally ill-fitting. The temptation to look inside was great, too strong to be resisted. The risk was slight, and he might learn something of value. At least, he would gain some idea of the kind of man Klaus Gerhardt was.

61

Merryck had learnt a lot about breaking and entering during his intelligence duties in the SAS, and he always carried with him a relic of those days – a pocket knife that looked perfectly ordinary, but in fact included a number of unusual – even illegal – gadgets. Gerhardt's lock took him about ninety seconds.

Once the door was open, Merryck paused, listening. No one was going up or down the stairs and, except for the sound of a crying child and the thump of a pop record, mercifully muted, the building seemed wrapped in a Sunday evening somnolence. Quickly, he pushed at the door and edged into the apartment.

The hall was really a passage, narrow and dark. Merryck didn't dare to switch on the light and he wished he'd brought a flashlight, and gloves. He waited for his eyes to adjust.

There were two doors on each side. One of those on the right was ajar, and Merryck pushed it wide. At once light from a street-lamp outside revealed the outlines of a kitchen, reasonably neat and tidy, but quite uninteresting.

The street-lamp helped to relieve the gloom of the passage, and he moved to his left, past a chair and a small table, to the door of what he assumed would be the living-room. In here he could see nothing – the darkness was impenetrable – and, guessing that shutters or heavy curtains shrouded the windows, he closed the door behind him and felt for the light switch.

This room, like the kitchen, appeared orderly. The furniture looked well-worn but not uncomfortable. There were a few books, some indifferent prints on the walls and in the place of honour on the mantel an ornate and rather ugly clock that had stopped at seven minutes past three. It was the room of a man who didn't care about the appearance of his surroundings as long as they were functional.

Merryck noted the thick dust on a table top. Clearly Klaus Gerhardt had been away for some time. But there was little dust on the shelves in front of the books, and one of the prints was askew.

Merryck put on the light, returned to the passage and tried the next door. This would be the bedroom, where he hoped there might be a desk of some kind. There had been no sign in the living-room of anywhere that papers could be kept. Again the darkness was opaque and, after shutting the door, Merryck switched on the light.

The bed was directly opposite him. It was a single bed, covered with what had once been a white counterpane. Now this was stained a rusty brown, the colour of dried blood. And on the bed, fully dressed, lay a small, elderly man with wispy grey hair and blue eyes which stared, unseeing, at the ceiling. He had been shot twice, through the head and the chest.

Slowly, swallowing the bile which rose in his throat, Merryck advanced across the room. He had never seen the little man before, but he had no doubt that this was Klaus Gerhardt. He touched the cold cheek, lifted the arm and let it fall. Gerhardt, he thought, had been dead some days, perhaps as long as a week. He could smell in the bedroom the faint, sweet odour of decay.

He looked around the simply furnished room. Again he found tell-tale signs. The religious picture over the bed was not quite straight. There was a layer of dust on the bedside table, but the top of the small desk with its double row of pigeon-holes was almost clean, and a piece of paper protruded from one of the drawers. The wardrobe, too, had not been properly shut.

Wrapping a handkerchief round his hand, Merryck opened desk drawers, chest of drawers, wardrobe. All had been subjected to a thorough, but probably hurried, search. If the varying layers of dust were to be accepted as evidence, it looked as if the killing had preceded the search by as much as several days, and it was a fair assumption that the killer and the searcher were not identical.

So once more it appeared that two people were ahead of him, Merryck thought grimly, and this time one of them had left solid proof that he wasn't playing games. Neither of them were amateurs. But nor was he, now that the rules were clear.

With great care Merryck retraced his steps, wiping everything he had touched. Inside the front door he waited in the dark passage. There was no light showing around the edges of the door, and no sound to be heard. The music had stopped. The child was no longer crying. As swiftly as he had entered, Merryck left the apartment.

He felt his way down the stairs and out of the building. Walking at a steady pace, he returned to his hotel, again making sure he had no tail. All was well on this occasion, but sooner or later Klaus Gerhardt's body would be found, all those in the apartments would be questioned, the routine would commence. And the West German criminal investigators were renowned for their thoroughness. If the boy who had been sent to buy bread described him with reasonable accuracy, if the police whom he'd encountered yesterday in the market recognized the description, if the nurse who had given him Gerhardt's address came forward – there could be trouble.

There was little likelihood that he would be accused of killing Klaus Gerhardt; he could prove he had only arrived in the Federal Republic on Friday and, if Gerhardt was found quite soon, forensic evidence would show the man had been dead days before that. But he could be apprehended, questioned, delayed. Colin Grenley would be far from happy.

The best thing he could do, Merryck decided, was to get out of the city. As soon as he'd talked to the priest tomorrow he'd push on to Berlin.

Punctually at eight-thirty the next morning Merryck was being shown into a parlour that smelt of sanctity and furniture polish. It was like Frau Schneider's apartment in that everything shone, even the lifesize wooden crucifix hanging on the far wall. Merryck sat down on a hard, rather uncomfortable settee, hoping he wouldn't have to wait long. The room was cold, and he shivered.

Within five minutes a priest appeared, followed by the housekeeper carrying a tray with two mugs of steaming coffee. Father Anselm introduced himself. He was a short, grey-haired man with a kind, weather-beaten face; he looked more like a farmer than a cleric. Kicking at the switch of an electric fire, he sat himself opposite Merryck.

'Now, Herr Merryck, what can I do for you?'

Merryck put his mug down slowly. 'How did you know my name?'

The priest's face creased in a broad smile. 'No magic, I promise. Frau Schneider gave me a good description of the third person to be interested in poor Martha Schmidt.'

'At least that should save me some explanation, Father.'

'Yes, mein Herr, you don't need to repeat the story you told Frau Schneider.'

The remark sounded perfectly innocent, but the priest's expression was a trifle too bland. Merryck warned himself not to underrate Father Anselm and, remembering that he'd mentioned to Frau Schneider that he would be leaving Bonn immediately, he said, 'In that case I'll try not to waste your time. Perhaps I shouldn't have bothered you at all. It was only on second thoughts that I decided to. Frau Schneider assured me Frau Schmidt had no close relations but, as you are her priest as well as her heir, it seemed to me wise to ask you to confirm that statement.'

'It is the church that inherits from Frau Schmidt, not I, Herr Merryck,' the priest corrected him, 'and I don't think either of us can help you.'

It was an ambiguous and interesting answer. Merryck wondered if Father Anselm had purposely avoided a direct lie. He asked bluntly, 'Did she never speak to you of her brother, Otto Krasner, the politician from the Democratic Republic?'

'She mentioned him on occasion, yes. I suppose he would have been her closest relation after her husband, as the

Schmidts were childless. But I take it you're only concerned with the living, Herr Merryck. As I said, I can't help you. So, if there's nothing else –' Father Anselm made to stand.

Merryck hesitated for only a moment. 'Did she tell you her brother was still alive, Father?'

It was the priest's turn to pause. He got to his feet and looked down at Merryck. He said, 'Herr Merryck, I was for many years Frau Schmidt's confessor. I don't need to tell you what that means. I think perhaps it's best if we don't continue this conversation.'

Merryck stood up reluctantly. 'Father would you tell me one thing then? Earlier you referred to me as the "third person". Has either of the others paid a call on you?'

'No. They were foolish or unlucky enough to tell Frau Schneider they were cousins of Martha Schmidt, and she didn't believe them, so she wasn't very helpful.' The priest smiled to take the sting out of his next words. 'Unlike me, she seems to have trusted you, Herr Merryck.'

'I'm sorry, Father.'

'If you could bring yourself to tell me the truth, I might be more inclined to help you.'

'It's not my story to tell.'

'In that case I can only wish you Godspeed.'

'Perhaps –' Merryck hesitated and the priest waited. 'If I were sure you would respect my confidence –'

'Unless you are about to confess to a crime or wish me to share some criminal knowledge, I give you my word, Herr Merryck. Your confidences will be safe with me.' Father Anselm resumed his seat and waved Merryck back to the settee.

'Thank you.' Merryck sat, his thoughts turning unwillingly to the murdered Klaus Gerhardt. After a moment he said, 'Father, I believe Martha Schmidt's brother, Otto, is still alive. I need to find him and talk to him. I swear I mean him no harm, but it's possible he has some vital information – information which might help to restore the tarnished reputation of a very eminent Englishman, and thus reaffirm my country's integrity. I hope that doesn't sound too – pompous – or absurd. It's the truth.'

The priest bowed his head, resting it on his hand so that his face was hidden from Merryck, who wondered if he were praying. For a full minute he said nothing. Then suddenly he looked up and nodded as if he had reached a decision.

He said, 'Frau Schmidt gave me a small package to be posted in the event of her death. I've done as she wished. I will give you the address, or such of it as I can remember. But I warn you, Herr Merryck, it may be of no help or relevance.'

'I understand that.'

'Very good. The package was addressed to a Madame Legros, rue de Longchamp, Neuilly, near Paris. I can't recall the street number. And that is all I can do for you.'

'Thank you very much, Father. *Danke. Danke schön.*'

Merryck hid his disappointment. The name and address sounded unlikely, for he couldn't believe Krasner was in Paris. More probably Madame Legros was the old school-friend of whom Frau Schneider had spoken. But, whoever she might be, she clearly had some close connection with Martha Schmidt. He decided to forget Berlin for the moment, and make straight for Paris.

Seven

———◆———

Hugh Merryck managed to get a seat on the Lufthansa Bonn – Paris flight that Monday evening. He kept an eye out for any sign of watchers, but made no attempt to hide his movements. He took the Air France bus from Charles de Gaulle airport to the Porte Maillot terminal, and then a taxi to the Inter-Continental Hotel near the corner of the rue de Castiglione and the rue de Rivoli. He had given his choice of hotel some thought. The Inter-Continental was expensive, luxurious and central, not the kind of place that would be picked by anyone with something to hide. On the other hand, it was large and relatively anonymous, a place where another foreigner would hardly be noticed. Further it had been modernized, and had all the facilities he might need. He had decided not to bother with a rented car in the city, but to rely on public transport and taxis.

As soon as he reached his room he examined the telephone directories on the desk. As he thought, Neuilly was not in the Paris books, and he called the concierge and asked for a copy of the Hauts-de-Seine Directory. In this he found only two Legros families. Both lived on the rue de Longchamp, a long street near the Pont de Neuilly Métro station.

The next morning Merryck walked its length, from the Avenue de Neuilly where, with its cluster of small shops, it had a village-like atmosphere, to the very edge of the Bois de Boulogne. One family Legros apparently lived in an elegant apartment block with view over the Bois, while the other occupied a much less imposing block just five minutes from the Avenue. He decided to try his luck there first and retraced his steps.

The entrance was under an archway. To the left were glass

doors revealing a lift and a flight of stairs, to the right the concierge's lodge. There was no list of names, nothing to indicate in which apartment Madame Legros might live. He was forced to ring the concierge's bell and enquire.

'*Deuxième étage, premier à gauche,*' he was told after a pair of elderly but intelligent eyes had scrutinized him carefully.

Merryck followed the instructions, climbed to the second floor and pushed the bell beside the first door on the left. As he waited he heard a small sound from inside the apartment, and he was sure he was again under scrutiny, this time through the little glass lens set into the middle of the door. Finally, the door was opened to him.

'*Bonjour, Madame. Madame Legros?*'

'*Oui.*'

She was quite different from what Merryck had expected, and certainly no former schoolfriend of Frau Schmidt. A tall girl, pretty, with light brown hair and blue eyes, Merryck guessed she was in her early twenties. She looked at him enquiringly.

'I'm sorry to bother you,' he said, automatically speaking French, 'but I wonder if you can help me. I'm trying to find –'

'Please, I don't understand.' The girl held up her hand, her French slow and careful. 'I do not speak French very well. Please speak more slowly.'

Merryck grinned at her. 'Would German be easier for you?' he asked in that language.

'What?' Her expression was blank.

'English then?'

'Oh, English would be just fine.' She smiled, showing very white teeth.

'You're an American,' Merryck said, amused. 'I'm afraid I was misled by your name.'

'My husband's French. I'm Canadian.' Proudly she pointed to the gold maple leaf at the neck of her dress which, loose-fitting though it was, did little to disguise the fact that she was expecting a child in two or three months' time.

'Anyway, what can I do for you?' she went on. 'I hope you're not trying to sell something.'

Merryck shook his head. 'No. I'm looking for a Madame Legros who lives in the rue de Longchamp, but somehow I don't think I've got the right one.'

'Well, there's another rue de Longchamp in the Sixteenth. Or perhaps you want my mother-in-law. She lives on this one, but down by the Bois.'

'It must be her,' said Merryck. 'I know she lives in Neuilly.'

'What do you want her for?'

'Do you know if she had a friend who lived in Bonn, a German woman – a Frau Schmidt – who was killed recently in a traffic accident?'

Merryck spoke casually. He expected an equally casual reply, not even the shut face that the mere mention of Frau Schmidt seemed to produce so often. He was completely unprepared for the girl's reaction. Her eyes widened, colour fled from her cheeks, her mouth opened. She took a step backwards, then another. Her knees buckled and she slid to the floor in a dead faint.

Merryck acted quickly. Stepping into the hall of the apartment, he kicked the front door shut behind him, picked up the young Madame Legros and carried her into the sitting-room where he laid her on a couch. She was already regaining consciousness. He fetched some water from the kitchen and supported her while she sipped it.

She opened her eyes quite soon, and Merryck smiled at her. 'I'm very sorry,' he said. 'I didn't mean to frighten you. I merely hoped that you or your mother-in-law might know Frau Schmidt.'

'No, I've never heard of her. And I'm sure my mother-in-law hasn't either.' Her colour had returned and she looked almost normal. She put her hand on her stomach. 'The baby kicked suddenly and I wasn't expecting it.'

Merryck took the glass from her and put it on a table. The girl had guts, he thought, and a quick brain, but he didn't rate her highly as a liar. He was certain the name of Martha Schmidt had meant something – perhaps a good deal – to her. In other circumstances he would have pressed her, questioned her further and more firmly, but the baby stopped him. Her faint at least had been genuine.

Telling himself he was getting sentimental, soft even, he said, 'Would you like me to telephone your husband or your doctor or –'

'No. I'm just fine now. Please go!'

Merryck glanced around the room. If her mother-in-law proved ignorant or uncommunicative he would have to return, and the more he knew about her the better. But the décor told him little. It seemed to be a haphazard mixture of tastes.

'Are you certain I shouldn't phone your husband?' he said doubtfully.

'Yes. Positive.' She swung her legs off the couch and stood up. 'You've been ever so kind, but please go. I've a lot of things to do.'

'Okay. And my apologies once more.'

Merryck let himself out of the apartment. The girl watched him go, but didn't move, made no attempt to see him to the door. Outside with the door closed, he immediately bent down, pretending to fiddle with his shoe, but keeping well below the field of vision of the spy-hole. Smiling grimly, he strained his ears to listen, and was at once rewarded.

As soon as she believed him gone, Madame Legros had wasted no time. She was already on the phone. It was impossible to hear what she was saying but, obviously agitated, she was speaking fast, almost certainly in English. Merryck wished he knew who was on the other end of the line. Not, he guessed, her husband – she had been too quick, too sharp in saying she didn't need him. And from the speed at which she spoke, probably not her French mother-in-law.

The lift creaked gently, warning of someone's approach. Merryck straightened and, without haste, walked down the stairs and out of the building.

In appearance, the other Madame Legros was as unlike her daughter-in-law as possible. She was short and dark, with enquiring brown eyes, large breasts and thin legs. She was encased in a flowered apron and, to judge from the delicious smells coming from the apartment, busy cooking.

'Yes, what is it? What do you want?' she asked abruptly. 'I hope you saw the notice, monsieur. Salesmen are not allowed in this building.'

'I'm not selling anything, madame,' Merryck gave her his most charming smile, and sniffed appreciatively. 'All the same, I'm afraid I'm disturbing you.'

'What is it then? You want money for yet another cause?'

'No, madame. In fact, I'm doing a survey for *France Soir*. It's on the French family.' Merryck lied fluently. 'I'm collecting statistics, and I have to call on every twentieth household in this street. I'd be very grateful if you could spare me a couple of minutes to answer some simple questions.'

'Well – I don't know.'

'Whatever you chose to tell me would be strictly confidential. We don't even record names and addresses.'

But Madame Legros didn't like the idea. She was beginning to shake her head when there was a sudden sizzling sound, and from the kitchen came the smell of something burning. Madame Legros ran, everything forgotten except for her *bœuf bourgignon*.

Uninvited, Merryck stepped into the hall, quietly shut the front door and followed. Madame Legros was kneeling on the floor, her head almost in the open oven. 'A damp cloth,' she demanded immediately. 'There, by the sink.'

Merryck fetched the cloth. The spillage was mopped up. The *bœuf* was saved. The emergency was over. But it had formed a kind of bond between them. Madame Legros stood up, regarded Merryck with some approval and sat down at the kitchen table. She pointed to a chair opposite.

'So, what are these questions, monsieur?'

Merryck had come prepared for this interview. From his

briefcase he produced a pad of lined paper, and he took out his pen. He began with innocuous questions, size of apartment, number of bathrooms, how many in family. One son was still living at home.

'You have other children, madame?'

'Yes, indeed. A son and two daughters. And three grand-children.'

'You have grandchildren?' Merryck forced himself to sound surprised.

'Yes.' Madame Legros beamed at him. 'A moment.'

She hurried from the kitchen and returned with a collection of framed photographs, which she proceeded to discuss in detail. Her main interest was in her grandchildren and Merryck had to curb his impatience until, at last, she produced the wedding photograph of her elder son and the girl to whom Merryck had been talking less than an hour ago. 'They're expecting a baby in June – my fourth grand-child,' she said proudly.

'Your daughter-in-law – how pretty she is,' Merryck said, handing back the photograph.

'Yes, I suppose Lotte is quite pretty,' Madame Legros agreed somewhat doubtfully.

'Lotte?' It was an excellent opening and Merryck seized upon it. 'Surely that's a German name. Is she German?'

'No, no!' Madame Legros shook her head violently. 'I was only a child in the last war, monsieur, but I remember my parents talking of it very well – very well indeed. If Pierre had brought home a German girl, I'd have disowned him. Lotte is a Canadian.'

'Of German stock, perhaps?'

Madame Legros shrugged. 'I doubt it. Before she married she was called Carlton, which is a very English name, is it not?'

'I think so,' Merryck said. 'Did they meet in Paris?'

'No, in New York. The firm sent Pierre to America for a year, and he found himself working in the same office as Martha Carlton, the elder sister – and that was that.'

Madame Legros made an expressive grimace. 'Through her he met her sister Lotte. They were married within a month, and he brought her home.'

Merryck opened his mouth to ask the name of the firm, but was forestalled by a warning buzzer on the stove. Immediately Madame Legros went into action. Merryck was now in her way.

'That's all, monsieur. I'm busy, as you can see. My husband and son will be returning soon, and they'll expect their dinner to be ready.'

Collecting her photographs, Madame Legros urged Merryck into the hall. When he stood his ground and asked where her sons worked she paid no attention. Her mind was on the meal she was about to serve.

'*Madame, je vous en prie,*' he pleaded. 'Just answer this one last question for me.'

'Jean is at school. He takes his *bac* this year,' she said impatiently. 'And Pierre works with his father, in Legros et fils, the wine exporters.'

The door was practically shut in Merryck's face while he was still expressing his thanks, but he didn't care. He had learnt far more than he expected from the Mesdames Legros. And surely he was on the right track. Everything pointed to it. Lotte Legros had almost certainly been upset when he mentioned Frau Schmidt. Then there were the names. Martha – after Aunt Martha? And Lotte – clearly German. In his letter Otto Krasner had written of two daughters, one of whom was soon to have a child. It could all be coincidence but, added to the connection that Father Anselm had provided, Merryck was prepared to bet that Lotte Carlton, now Lotte Legros, had once been Lotte Krasner.

As he walked slowly eastwards along the boulevard that edged the Bois, Merryck considered his next move. He could return to the younger Madame Legros and question her further, hoping she would admit her parentage, knew where her father was, and would co-operate. Or he could contact the other sister in New York. Instinct told Merryck that the key to the matter lay in America – the CIA were highly unlikely to have concealed Krasner in Europe – and that, with the lead he now had, he should get there soon. His mind made up, he began to search for a taxi.

Back in his hotel room, once he judged the midday meal period was over, Merryck set to work on the phone. Fortunately the hotel was equipped with direct-dial instruments, so he had no need to go through an operator, even for overseas calls.

In the Paris Directory he found Henri Legros et fils, wine merchants. He dialled the number and asked for Monsieur Pierre. He gave his name as Hank Cuthbertson, from New York City.

After a moment a man came on the line. 'Monsieur Cuther-bertson? This is Pierre Legros.'

'Pierre! Great to hear your voice again. How are you? Long time no see.' Merryck, trusting that the telephone would disguise the deficiencies in his American accent, tried to sound as hearty as he could. 'How's business? Flourishing?'

'Yes, thank you. Business is flourishing. And I – I'm fine.' Pierre Legros sounded hesitant, clearly trying to place Hank Cuthbertson. 'How are you, monsieur?'

'I'm fine, just fine. But what's this "monsieur" nonsense?' Merryck laughed. 'Say, Pierre, you do remember me, don't you?'

'But of course, Hank.'

Grinning to himself at this blatant untruth, Merryck said, 'I used to visit that firm of yours about once a month. What did they call it?'

'You mean in New York? De Gruchy and Grand?'

'Sure. My memory! I'd forget my head if it wasn't stuck on.' Merryck laughed again. 'Well, Pierre, I've got to go. I'm only passing through, and they're calling my flight. Nice talking to you. Look me up if you get to the US of A. I'm based in Chicago presently. 'Bye now.'

Pleased, Merryck put down the receiver. The next thing was to check on Martha. He was pretty sure the hotel concierge would have a New York City phone book, but he was reluctant to reveal his interest in De Gruchy and Grand. Instead, he got the number he wanted – and an address on New York's Sixth Avenue – by speaking directly to international directory enquiries.

Once more Merryck lifted the receiver and dialled. He heard the distinctive North American ringing tone and waited till a voice answered, 'De Gruchy and Grand. Can I help you?'

'Miss Martha Carlton, please.'

'One moment, sir.' The American voice might have been in the next room.

There was a click, and a pleasant, slightly husky voice spoke in his ear. 'Martha Carlton here.'

Merryck quickly tapped the receiver twice with his fingernail, and put it down. With any luck Martha Carlton would think a call had been cut off in error.

So now Merryck had everything he needed – except a visa for the States. Once more he reached for the phone. After fighting his way through the bureaucracy, and eventually reaching a senior official of the US consular staff, he was dismayed to discover that it would take the whole of one day to acquire this essential. He thought of calling the British Embassy to intercede on his behalf, but remembered that his connection with the FCO was, at best, tenuous.

He had one more call to make – to the number that Colin Grenley had given him. So far he'd not used it, but he got through without difficulty, and a girl's voice said noncommittally, 'Mr Grenley's office.'

Merryck identified himself, and asked to be put through to Grenley.

The voice became more animated. 'I'm sorry, Colin's in Geneva. But we've been expecting to hear from you, Mr Merryck. Where are you? Still in Bonn?'

Remembering Grenley's instructions, Merryck confined

himself to essentials. 'No. I'm in Paris. You can take a message?'

'Yes, easily. Or he can call you back.'

Merryck hesitated, considering. 'No, there's no need for that. Just tell him I'm making progress, and I'll be leaving for New York in the next day or two, as soon as I can get a visa.'

The clerk called, 'Mr Merryck!'

Merryck's response was slow. He was bored and restless, and he'd heard so many names called in the last two hours that he scarcely recognized his own.

He had arrived at the Visa Section of the US Embassy in the rue St Florentin – just a couple of blocks from his hotel – as the doors of the office were opening that morning, filled in his application form and delivered it with his passport into the hands of the American authorities. He'd been told to return late in the afternoon, but in his anxiety had arrived soon after lunch, and waited. The motley collection of people that flowed through the place was at first not uninteresting, creating as it did an atmosphere of bustle, expectancy, confusion, even helplessness. But this spectacle soon palled, and Merryck merely sat resignedly.

'Mr Merryck!'

The call sounded slightly aggrieved. The office would soon be closing, and the clerk was impatient. Merryck hurried to the wicket. As he received his passport with its new visa, he was aware of another man behind the clerk, inspecting him closely.

So what? he thought. At least they're not prepared to refuse me permission to land. He'd already booked a seat on tomorrow's TWA flight, and now had only to collect his ticket.

Eight

'I'd like to speak to Miss Martha Carlton, please,' Merryck said into the phone.

'Who shall I say is calling, sir?'

As he waited, gazing from the window of his room on the twenty-second floor of the Barbizon Plaza across the trees of Central Park, Merryck felt a prickle of excitement. A lot could depend on Martha Carlton. If she were prepared to co-operate, she might make his job a whole lot easier. Because the more he thought about it – and he'd had plenty of time to think as the TWA Jumbo carried him across the Atlantic – the more convinced he became that he was getting closer to Otto Krasner.

'Mr Merryck? Martha Carlton.'

'Hello, Miss Carlton. You won't know my name – Hugh Merryck. But we've got a mutual friend – Johnny Davidson. It's my first visit to New York, and he suggested I should get in touch with you. I do hope you don't mind.'

'Why no, Mr Merryck.' Her voice held a hint of amusement. 'But who did you say? A Johnny Davidson?'

'He's in the wine business. Please don't tell me you can't remember him, Miss Carlton. That would be awfully embarrassing,' Merryck said hurriedly.

She laughed. 'I can't recall him right now, Mr Merryck, but one meets a lot of people. There's no need to be embarrassed.'

'There is, you know. I was going to ask you – on the strength of Johnny's introduction, as it were – if you'd have a drink with me after work. That is, if you're not doing anything else. I don't know a soul in New York City and –'

There was only the slightest hesitation before Martha Carlton agreed. Merryck arranged to pick her up at her office, which was only eight or nine short blocks from his hotel, down Sixth Avenue – now known officially, he had already discovered, as the Avenue of the Americas.

He had plenty of time, so he decided to walk. It really was his first visit to New York City and, instead of taking a direct path, he strolled over to Fifth Avenue and eventually crossed back, alongside the Rockefeller Center, to the towering building, all glass and steel, that housed the offices of De Gruchy and Grand.

It was an exhilarating walk in the sunny but cool early evening. Forgotten were the stories he'd heard and read of murders and muggings, assaults and rapes, and the bankrupt state of the city. Merryck was entranced by its vitality, its urgency, its purposefulness. He arrived at his destination in a state of high expectation.

De Gruchy and Grand occupied a suite of offices on the seventeenth floor of their block. Merryck asked for Miss Carlton, and was told she would be with him in a few minutes. He sat in the reception area – glass-walled on two sides and containing an over-abundance of house plants – and contemplated the antics of the tropical fish in a very large aquarium that stretched along the wall behind the receptionist's desk. Apart from a discreet list of vineyards and brand names, there was nothing to indicate that he was in the offices of a firm of wine importers.

Martha Carlton didn't keep him long. 'Mr Merryck?' she said as she came towards him.

Hugh Merryck got swiftly to his feet and took the hand that was offered. It was slim and cool, but the clasp was firm. To Merryck, at this first meeting, it seemed to personify the girl standing before him.

Martha Carlton was tall, with the same light brown hair and blue eyes as her sister. But whereas Lotte was pretty and appealing even in her pregnancy, Martha was composed and beautiful. And, he guessed, very efficient. As they left and

Martha said good-night to the receptionist, he noticed that the girl addressed her formally as Miss Carlton.

'Are you a very senior executive in De Gruchy and Grand?' he asked as they walked towards the elevators.

'Not yet,' Martha Carlton said calmly. 'Presently I'm personal assistant to the president, which carries a certain amount of status, but not necessarily a big pay check. I'm still learning the business. What do you do, Mr Merryck? Are you in the liquor trade too?'

'Oh no. Nothing like that. I'm in the legal business. I'm over here doing a small job for a colleague who couldn't get away. And my name's Hugh, Miss Carlton.'

'Mine's Martha, as you know.' Again there was that slightly amused, faintly ironical note in her voice. 'And where's your home town, Hugh?'

Telling himself not to underrate this girl, Merryck stayed as close to the truth as possible. 'My parents live in the Isle of Wight, but I've been around a good deal. Actually, I used to be in the army – the British army – but soldiering wasn't for me. It was hard on my father when I decided to quit. We've always been a military family . . .'

Martha had recommended a bar just off Sixth Avenue and as they strolled towards it Merryck talked on, about his brothers and his family and their life in England. His words sounded casual, friendly. But he was watching every sentence, and none was without purpose. He hoped he was casting bread upon favourable water.

They were sitting opposite each other in a pleasant bar, dimly-lit like all such places in the States, when he asked a leading question.

'And now, what about you, Martha? Where does your family hail from?'

'We're Canadians originally, born and bred in Ontario. But we've lived in the United States for years. I've even thought of taking out naturalization papers, but my parents are against it.'

'They live here in New York?'

'In the State, yes. Not in the City. In Westchester County, north of Manhattan. You might call it a suburb. Dad commutes from there every day.'

'He hasn't retired?' Merryck was careful not to sound surprised.

'Heavens, no. I don't think Dad'll ever retire. He runs his own advertising agency over on Madison Avenue, and he's a genuine workaholic. He wanted my brother to join him in the firm, but –'

'Your brother?' Once again Merryck hid his surprise. Otto Krasner's letter to Martha Schmidt had implied that he was in no fit state for hard work, and it certainly hadn't mentioned a son. But people did work with heart conditions, and it had been a relatively brief note, perhaps only intended to convey the latest items of family news. Still, it was puzzling.

'Yes,' Martha was saying. 'I've got a sister, Lotte, who lives in France, and a brother, Ken, who's at the Juilliard School up in Lincoln Center. He comes in with Dad three or four times a week.'

'The Juilliard School. That's a music academy, isn't it?'

'Sure. My brother's a fine pianist.'

'I see,' said Merryck slowly. He changed the subject, and they continued to chat, seemingly enjoying each other's company. But when Merryck offered her another drink, Martha Carlton glanced at her watch and said she must go, she had a date. Merryck expressed regret.

'I'm sorry. I was hoping you might have dinner with me.'

'I'm sorry too. It's real nice of you to ask me.'

'What about tomorrow?'

'Tomorrow's Friday, and I usually go home at weekends. My mother likes to see one of her daughters regularly, and she misses Lotte now she's so far away. For that matter, so do I. There's only eighteen months between us, and we're very close.'

Merryck wondered for a moment if this was meant to be some kind of warning, a signal not to ask more questions, not

81

to probe too deeply. He'd noticed that Martha hadn't queried the mutual friend he'd invented, and as they came out of the bar he said, a little tentatively, 'I'm terribly grateful to Johnny Davidson for serving as an introduction, even if you don't remember him. When can I see you again?'

Once more that slight smile passed across Martha's face, but she made no direct comment on Davidson. Instead she said, 'That depends on how long you're going to be in New York.'

'I'm not sure. The chap I've got to see is out of town, and won't be back till Monday.'

'Too bad.'

'Yes. I'd hoped you –' Merryck grinned resignedly.

Martha Carlton waved at a passing cab. As it drew up beside them with a squeal, she said suddenly, 'Look, I wonder – you might find it pretty dull, but if you don't want to spend the weekend alone in the city, why not come home with me. I usually drive up on Friday and back on Sunday afternoon.'

Merryck was delighted. 'That's awfully kind of you. It would be wonderful! Great! But – what about your parents?'

'They'd love to meet you, Hugh. Why not?'

Without waiting for an answer she murmured an address to the cab driver, opened the door, got in and wound down the window. 'I'll pick you up at your hotel around a quarter of five tomorrow evening. The Barbizon Plaza, you said? Be at the Central Park South entrance. Okay?'

'I'll be waiting,' Merryck said. 'And thanks a lot.'

Merryck watched the cab draw away and merge into the uptown traffic. He waved, but Martha Carlton didn't turn. Standing on the edge of the sidewalk he stared speculatively after her, even when he could no longer see the taxi. Then someone jostled him and, even though it was growing noticeably colder, he began to walk slowly back to his hotel.

He found it hard to believe his luck, that he'd actually been invited to spend the weekend with the Carltons. It had all been too simple, Martha too trusting, too many obvious questions left unasked. Or was he being overly suspicious?

He paused on the edge of a kerb, waiting for the red 'Don't Walk' sign to change. There had been no time for a letter from Lotte to reach her sister, and maybe Lotte hadn't thought it necessary to phone to warn Martha of the Englishman and his interest in Frau Schmidt. It was always possible he was merely experiencing the American hospitality of which he'd heard so much – but not, Hugh Merryck told himself, very probable.

At about a quarter past four the following afternoon Merryck came down to the hotel lobby and told the clerk on duty that he'd be away for a couple of nights, but wanted to hold his room. Going over to the news-stand, he looked idly at the racks of magazines and paperbacks and American and foreign newspapers. A copy of *Die Welt* caught his eye. It was dated the day before yesterday, and he bought it and took it to a seat.

He glanced through its pages. There was nothing of particular interest to him, but in a desultory fashion he began to read a feature on the thriving European trade in lost and stolen passports. His mind was nine-tenths occupied with thoughts of Martha Carlton and the weekend ahead, and he was looking at his watch for the umpteenth time when he saw a short paragraph tucked away in an obscure corner of the page.

BONN GOVERNMENT SERVANT BRUTALLY MURDERED, the headline said. Klaus Gerhardt had been found. Merryck's attention was suddenly concentrated, but there was little to be learnt. Gerhardt's body had been discovered at the beginning of the week by workmen who had been let into the apartment for a routine check on the central heating. The police were making enquiries. If they had any clues they hadn't confided them to the reporter. Of course *Die Welt* was published in Hamburg. Perhaps a Cologne paper would have a fuller story, but –

'There you are,' a voice said, interrupting his train of

thought. 'Are you ready, Hugh? I'm double-parked, and the doorman's not too happy about it.'

'Martha! I'm terribly sorry. I meant to be waiting out-side.'

Merryck was on his feet, throwing down his newspaper, picking up his bag and briefcase. He gestured for Martha to go ahead of him. He hoped she hadn't noticed the German paper but suspected that she had.

He was sure of it when she said, 'Don't you want your newspaper, Hugh?'

'No, I've seen all I want,' he said lightly, and volunteered no more.

Martha didn't persist. She led the way out of the hotel, smiling her thanks at the doorman, who hurried to help them into a bright red coupé. Like yesterday, the weather was clear and bright, though cool, and Merryck did up his seat-belt and relaxed. He had little doubt that Martha would prove an efficient driver, and she was. She drove with great competence and authority, down two blocks to Fifty-Seventh Street, across Manhattan to the West Side Highway. It wasn't until they were moving northwards in a stream of traffic on the Henry Hudson Parkway that he realized how silent she'd been and how tense she was.

At first he put this down to his presence, and perhaps anxiety at the coming weekend. Then he saw how often she kept glancing at her rear-view mirror. On the pretext of turning to stare back at the great span of the George Washington Bridge across the Hudson River, he made a swift appraisal of the vehicles immediately behind them. The traffic had thinned slightly, and there were only about half a dozen cars near by. None was particularly distinctive, but Merryck did his best to make a mental note of them. Martha wasn't driving at the posted speed limit, and a couple of the cars overtook her very soon. She continued to use her mirror more frequently than was justified by the conditions.

'Something bothering you?' Merryck asked casually at last.

'Oh no. I was just wondering if I recognized a friend's car, that's all.'

Merryck accepted the explanation, though he didn't entirely believe it. But Martha took the implied hint, and began to chat, pointing out places of interest on their route – the northern tip of Manhattan Island, Van Cortland Park in the Bronx, the New York City line, where they crossed into Westchester and the divided highway became the Saw Mill River Parkway.

Three or four miles further north, Martha changed lanes, slowed and left the freeway. A blue Ford followed them through the exit, and hooted twice. Martha hooted in response.

'I was right,' she said, giving Merryck a pleased smile. 'It was Steve – Steve Ross. He's a neighbour of ours, and a good friend.'

'What does he do?' Merryck asked idly.

'He's in the insurance business. I expect you'll meet him. He usually visits with us on a weekend.'

Merryck made a noncommittal noise. It could be imagination, but it seemed to him that a lot of her earlier tension had left Martha as soon as she knew that this Steve Ross was around. He wondered about their relationship, and hoped the man wasn't going to interfere with his plans.

'Here we are,' Martha said some five minutes later. 'Welcome to Acacia Drive.'

They had turned into a quiet road, tree-lined, with big houses set well back behind manicured lawns and carefully-planted shrubs. The properties were not divided by hedges or fences, as they might have been in England, but by wide driveways leading to two- or three-car garages. The houses themselves were mostly of clapboard, with tiled roofs of various colours – colours that were often repeated in their front doors and trim. To judge from their size, the area of land each seemed to occupy, the number of expensive cars in the driveways and the general air of tidiness and prosperity, this was a high-income district.

The blue Ford drove by slowly as Martha and Merryck got out of the coupé beside one of the larger houses. A voice called, 'See you later, sweetie!' A hand waved.

'Hi, Steve!' Martha waved in return. She swung round to Merryck. 'Come along,' she said lightly, smiling. 'I don't know about you, Hugh, but I could do with a drink.'

'That sounds an excellent idea,' he said, grinning in response and, as he followed her to the front door, he wished this could have been the ordinary, friendly weekend that on the surface it seemed.

Nine

Martha Carlton ushered Merryck into a wide and pleasantly warm hall. 'Hi!' she shouted. 'It's me. Anybody home?'

A bell pinged as a telephone receiver was replaced, and a woman appeared through an open archway to the left. 'Hello, darling.' She kissed Martha fondly on both cheeks, then turned. 'You must be Hugh? How are you? I'm Peggy Carlton.' She held out a hand.

Merryck shook it and smiled. 'I think I'd have guessed that. How do you do, Mrs Carlton? It's awfully good of you to invite me.'

Peggy Carlton had light brown hair and blue eyes. Except that she was plump, she was very like Martha. She looked a kind and attractive woman, with laughter lines by her eyes and mouth, and Merryck took to her on sight. He reckoned that she was in her late forties, some twenty years younger than Otto Krasner – a not unduly surprising gap in ages.

'It's a pleasure,' she was saying. 'First, Martha'll show you up to the guest suite. Then when you come down we'll all have a drink. We won't wait for Dad.'

'Is Mr Carlton going to be late?' asked Merryck.

'Probably yes. He just called to say an important client's turned up out of the blue and he may have to entertain him in town. But let's hope not.'

Merryck managed to hide his disappointment at her words, though it looked as if he might not be meeting Martha's father tonight after all. But the old boy couldn't stay away the whole weekend. If he did, what was the point of arranging this invitation?

As such thoughts chased through Merryck's mind, he followed Martha up the stairs. She opened a door a little way along a corridor, and waved him into a bedroom. 'There's a bathroom through there,' she said. 'I hope you'll find everything you need. If not, give a shout.'

'Thanks a lot, Martha.'

'I'll be a few minutes. Just go down when you're ready. We have no help in the house at weekends, so we look after ourselves.'

'Fine. Okay.'

It was a pleasant room, overlooking a well-tended garden, but it was quite impersonal, obviously reserved for guests. Merryck noticed that the towels were monogrammed with a 'C', and thought wryly that he could scarcely have expected to find a 'K'. When he was ready he took the gift-wrapped box of English imported chocolates he had brought for his hostess, and opened his bedroom door.

Immediately he could hear the sound of someone playing the piano, playing extremely well. He went downstairs slowly and paused in the hall, listening, until Martha came running down behind him. She had changed from the severe suit she had been wearing into a loose-fitting caftan of some gold-coloured material and, distracted from the music, Merryck let his admiration show.

Martha ignored his look. 'He's great, isn't he?' she said. 'We're all awfully proud of him. Come and meet him.'

Merryck followed Martha through another archway into the living-room. Peggy Carlton was lying on a settee in front of a big log fire, her eyes shut as she listened to the music. The maker of the music was a broad-shouldered young man who continued to play, oblivious of their presence, until his piece was finished and the two women clapped.

He swung round on the piano stool. 'Hi!' he said, smiling at Martha and staring at Merryck.

'My brother, Ken,' Martha said. 'Ken, this is Hugh Merryck, our house-guest for the weekend.'

'Ah, the Limey.' Ken Carlton grinned, but didn't rise from his stool or offer to shake hands.

Merryck said, 'That was terrific. Bach, wasn't it?'

'Yes. One of the Preludes and Fugues,' Ken Carlton said briefly.

Mrs Carlton intervened quickly. 'Didn't Martha tell you? Ken's studying at the Juilliard School in the city. He's going to be a concert pianist one of these days. Aren't you, honey?'

'Maybe.'

It was an ungracious response and Merryck, sensing a certain latent hostility on Ken's part, looked at the young man with added interest. He was dark with brown eyes, and not in the least like Martha or Lotte or Peggy Carlton. It was difficult to believe he was so closely related to the three women.

For the moment, however, Merryck was given no chance to consider the problem. Martha was asking what people would like to drink, and she and Ken went off together. Mrs Carlton patted the settee beside her.

'Come and sit down, Hugh, and tell me about yourself. Are you married?'

It was, Merryck thought with a flash of humour, a typical mother's question. 'No,' he said. 'I'm not married,' and he presented her with the chocolates. 'Someday maybe.'

Mrs Carlton didn't press the point. Instead, she merely nodded understandingly and thanked Merryck for his gift. Then she began to talk of England. They hadn't been to Europe for several years, she said, but they planned to go in the fall. She and her husband were eager to see their first grandchild. Of course she wished Lotte had married an American – or preferably a Canadian. 'But there you are, you can't decide who your children'll marry.' She laughed.

'You've a very talented son,' Merryck said, probing a little.

'My chosen one? Yes.' Her smile was warm.

'Why do you call him that?'

'Because we did choose him, my husband and I. After Lotte I couldn't have any more children, but we wanted a son so we adopted Ken. Of course, at that time we didn't know we were taking on a prodigy.'

89

Before Merryck could make any comment the 'prodigy' returned, carrying a tray of drinks, and Martha followed him. Conversation became general: weather, sport, politics, the Royal Family – evidently a topic of intense fascination to Peggy Carlton at least – the British television programmes that were proving so popular on the PBS Network in the United States, and finally the question of supper. Mrs Carlton decided they would wait no longer for Dad.

'I'll leave something in the oven and, if he's not eaten in town, he can have it when he gets home,' she said firmly. 'We'll eat now. Come along.'

At the dining table, waiting to be served, Merryck found himself seated opposite a large oil painting of two small girls. He regarded it with interest. Though the execution was amateurish, the artist had caught something of the innocent happiness of childhood and it was a charming study.

'You can guess who they are?' Ken Carlton asked. 'Martha and Charlotte – at a tender age.'

'Charlotte?'

'He means Lotte, Martha's younger sister.' Mrs Carlton set a bowl of soup in front of Merryck. 'She was christened Charlotte after her godmother, but she soon shortened it to Lotte. I was quite pleased. It's much prettier than something like Charlie for a girl, don't you agree?'

Merryck nodded absently. He was thinking that it was a most interesting explanation for the German name, though it was certainly not one that had been volunteered by Madame Legros in Paris.

The meal progressed. The food was good, if a little unexciting, and there was a bottle of fine Californian wine. The telephone rang as Martha brought in a fruit pie.

Ken, who had jumped up to answer the call, returned saying, 'That was Dad. He's got to take this guy out on the town, so he'll be late home and we're not to wait up for him.'

Mrs Carlton clicked her tongue against the roof of her mouth in irritation. 'Poor Bill!' she said. 'That's too bad. He works quite hard enough during the week without having his weekends ruined.'

Merryck made sympathetic noises. If the Carlton family were playing games, he didn't really mind. The more petty obstructions that emerged to come between him and his meeting with 'Bill Carlton', the more convinced he became that he was on the right track, that Otto Krasner was within touching distance. And in the long run the confrontation was inevitable; the most ingenious ploys could do no more than postpone it.

Merryck accepted a second helping of pie, and said how good it was. Martha, he thought, was being rather quiet, but Peggy Carlton talked enough for two. The telephone rang again as they finished the meal and Ken went to answer it, as the two women began to clear the table. Merryck, his offer of help waved away, wandered into the living-room. He had noticed photographs on the mantel and others on a side-table, and was glad of a chance to look at them closely – not that he expected them to be very enlightening.

They were, as he expected, family photographs. There were studio portraits of the two girls and of Mrs Carlton, some wedding photographs – Lotte and her groom coming out of a church; Martha in an obvious bridesmaid's dress flanked by four small girls carrying little flower baskets – and a graduation picture of the adopted Ken looking serious in cap and gown. The rest were all amateur colour prints and included people he couldn't place. None of them was recognizable as Otto Krasner.

Martha brought in the coffee. Ken wanted to know if Merryck played bridge. Mrs Carlton returned from the phone to complain about a widowed neighbour who was always calling at inconvenient moments. And the rest of the evening passed pleasantly with casual chat and several rubbers of bridge. At midnight they went to bed.

Merryck slept peacefully, to be woken by a pale sun shining on his face. It was after eight and, hopeful of breakfast, he showered, shaved, dressed and went downstairs. Guided by the smell of coffee, he found his way to a spacious, modern kitchen. Mrs Carlton and Martha, both in housecoats, were seated at a breakfast bar, chatting across their coffee mugs.

They greeted Merryck warmly, asked how he'd slept and what he'd like to eat. Ken poked his head round the door and said he'd be off, he'd see them all later. Mrs Carlton explained that his girl-friend lived not far away, and he spent most of his free time at her house. She winced as the front door slammed.

'That boy!' she said. 'He'll wake his father.'

'Mr Carlton got back last night then?' Merryck said, biting into a piece of toast.

'Yes, but not till after two, so he's sleeping in this morning.'

Martha smiled. 'You must have slept well if you didn't hear Dad come in. He made much more noise than Ken does.'

'Your father doesn't have as much practice at returning in the small hours,' Peggy Carlton said reprovingly.

Merryck laughed. 'You sound like my mother,' he said. 'It makes me feel very much at home.'

They laughed with him, and Merryck thought ruefully that he'd spoken the truth. Mrs Carlton did make him feel at home. But Martha, he sensed, was again very tense, perhaps because her father was now in the house. He wondered how long it would be before the man was prepared to meet him.

As if reading his mind Mrs Carlton said, 'Well, I'm sure it's good for Bill to rest. But how are you two going to occupy yourselves today?'

'I thought we might drive across the Hudson and up to Albany on the Thruway, perhaps get as far as Saratoga,' Martha said. For Merryck's benefit, she added, 'Albany's the State Capital, and Saratoga Springs is a kind of horse-racing centre. They're both quite interesting. Then we could come back off the main highways. You could see the Mohawk Valley and the Catskills – that's a favourite resort

92

area for New Yorkers. How does that sound?'

'Wonderful.' said Merryck. 'but isn't it going to take all day?'

'Most of it, yes.'

'Don't be too late home, dear. Remember the Bensons are coming to supper tonight – and Steve, I hope.'

'No, we won't, Mom.'

Mrs Carlton pushed back her seat, and began to collect the dirty dishes and stack them in the dishwasher. 'Have a good day,' she said.

It was a good day. A day to remember, Hugh Merryck told himself as he showered before dinner. It would have been perfection, if only it hadn't been shadowed by the sense that he was being deliberately kept from Otto Krasner. He wondered what excuse would be made this evening for the non-appearance of the master of the house.

Downstairs he once more found Ken playing the piano, this time a Chopin Etude, but without an admiring audience. Mrs Carlton was bustling in and out of the living-room, bringing bowls of nuts and plates of canapés, calling instructions to Martha, who was busy in the kitchen. It was a very ordinary, pleasant scene, probably being re-enacted in hundreds of similar houses throughout Westchester County.

The front door chimes sounded and Mrs Carlton hurried into the hall. Merryck heard a man's voice. 'God, it's turned chilly tonight. The thermometer's dropped fifteen degrees in the last hour. I only hope we're not going to have another snowfall.'

He came into the living-room, a tall man in his mid-thirties with dark hair receding at the temples, craggy features and cold, grey eyes. He waved a hand at Ken, who missed a couple of bars to raise a hand in return, but didn't stop playing. Mrs Carlton introduced the newcomer to Merryck.

'This is our friend and neighbour, Steve Ross. He lives just a couple of blocks away.'

93

They scarcely had time to shake hands before Martha came in. At once Ross enfolded her in his arms, and kissed her affectionately. 'And how's my girl tonight?'

'Fine, Steve. And you?'

The door chimes sounded again. 'Oh, where is Bill?' Mrs Carlton said. 'He was ready a half hour ago.'

'He went down to the basement,' Ken said. 'He's finding some wine.'

Ross released Martha. 'I'll go get Bill,' he said. 'You let in your other guests before they freeze.'

The piano played softly as Merryck stood with his back to the fire, waiting, containing his rising excitement. Almost immediately there was a babble of voices from the hall, the sound of greetings, kisses. The living-room, large as it was, suddenly seemed full of people. Martha had disappeared into the kitchen, but Mrs Carlton had returned with Steve Ross and three others, all strangers to Merryck.

'This is Hugh Merryck, who's visiting with us from England,' Mrs Carlton introduced him. 'Agnes and Perry Benson.'

'How are you, Mr Merryck?'

They were a couple in their fifties, grey-haired, expensively dressed, eager to be friendly. They shook hands, asked him how he liked New York. Ken stopped playing and came to greet them. And the man whom Merryck had not yet met came forward, his hand held out.

'Hugh,' he said, 'I'm Bill Carlton. I'm very sorry we've not managed to get together before this, but I've been kind of occupied, what with one thing and another. You know how it is.' He gave Merryck a wide grin and a firm handshake. 'Anyway, it's good to meet you now.'

'I'm glad to meet you too, sir.'

Merryck's voice was level and, he hoped, not obviously lacking in sincerity. Somehow he managed to force his face muscles into an answering smile. But the smile didn't reach his eyes. He had recognized Bill Carlton as someone who appeared often in the photographs he'd inspected so carefully the previous evening, someone he'd assumed to be a family friend.

And someone who could not possibly be Otto Krasner. This man was in his late forties or early fifties, fair-haired, blue-eyed, with the physique of an American football player. Hair dye, make-up, even plastic surgery – nothing could have transformed a sick sixty-eight-year-old German into this clearly genuine picture of natural good health and relative youth.

Then who was Bill Carlton? Peggy Carlton claimed him as her husband, Martha and Ken as their father. More importantly, Ross and the Bensons accepted him. If he had been substituted for Otto Krasner, there must have been a complex conspiracy. From the way Ross couldn't keep his eyes off Martha, Merryck guessed he would have done the Carltons almost any favour, but the Bensons seemed unlikely plotters.

While his thoughts rioted, Merryck drank the gin and tonic that Ken had brought him, and made conversation with Agnes Benson. They talked about England, which she seemed to know well, and about her family and Merryck's. Like many Americans, Mrs Benson was only too pleased to disclose her life history; a few simple questions elicited the information that her husband was in the same line of business as Bill Carlton, and that the two families had been close friends for years – ever since the Carltons had moved down from Canada, in fact. Her story sounded totally convincing.

Throughout dinner and for the rest of the evening Merryck listened intently, but he heard no false note, received no hint that Carlton was other than he seemed to be – husband, father, friend. There was too much ease between them all, too much shared knowledge, for it to be reasonable to believe that Bill Carlton was some substitute who had taken Krasner's place for the evening, and that the rest of the party was conniving at a charade.

Nevertheless, Merryck assured himself, some connection

must exist between Frau Schmidt, Krasner's sister, and Lotte Legros, born Charlotte Carlton. There was no reason on earth – or in heaven – for Father Anselm to invent the story of the package Martha Schmidt had entrusted to him for transmission to Lotte; what the priest had said must be taken as indisputable fact.

The next morning when he came downstairs, he found Martha and her parents discussing the weather. It hadn't snowed in the night, but outside it was grey and bitterly cold. Mrs Carlton remarked that they normally had brunch after church on Sundays, and perhaps it was the memory of Father Anselm that made Merryck offer to go to church with them. It was an ordinary enough suggestion but, for the first time since his arrival at their house, he was aware of really disconcerting his host and hostess.

Bill Carlton recovered his aplomb almost at once. 'You surprise me, Hugh,' he said lightly. 'I don't expect young people to be churchgoers these days. None of our children go, I'm sorry to say – it's just Peggy and me.'

'I always go when I'm at home,' Merryck lied.

'But that's Church of England, isn't it? I – I'm not sure you'd like our service, Hugh.' Peggy Carlton was quick, perhaps too quick.

Merryck, intrigued by the Carltons' seeming reluctance to take him with them, merely smiled and, even when Martha intervened to suggest music or table tennis in the playroom, he resisted the temptation to spend the morning with her. She shrugged irritably. 'I didn't realize you were religious, Hugh,' she said, almost as if she'd suddenly learnt he had some dread disease.

But Merryck was not to be deterred, and soon found himself sitting between the Carltons on the front seat of a long, wide Cadillac. Then there was a pause while Mrs Carlton went back to the house to retrieve her forgotten purse. Bill Carlton shrugged. 'Women!' he said resignedly. Merryck made a sympathetic noise and commented on the efficiency of the car's heater. It was, as Peggy had said, very cold, and he was unprotected in his thin raincoat.

The delay ensured that they were late in arriving at the church – an austere but pleasant building. As they hurried through the parking lot, Merryck saw a sign which proclaimed the denomination as 'Episcopalian'. Surely, he thought, that's the American equivalent of Church of England. Was it likely that Peggy Carlton didn't know? The vague disquiet aroused by this question was however soon allayed. Two or three people smiled welcomes as they found seats together in a rear pew, and at the end of the service the parson greeted the Carltons by name as he stood in the porch shaking hands with the members of his departing congregation.

'Bill, Peggy,' he said, 'how good to see you. I'm going to give you a call some day soon. It's not too early to start thinking of the annual bazaar, and I'll want your help as usual.'

'Fine,' Bill Carlton said. 'You can rely on us.'

'Come to supper,' Mrs Carlton added.

They apologized to Merryck for not introducing him, but the congestion in the small porch made conversation difficult. Outside, they hurried to the car, and the temperature made Merryck glad they didn't stop to chat with friends.

Bill Carlton started the engine. Then suddenly a woman knocked imperiously on the window on Peggy's side of the car. Bill Carlton groaned aloud. Peggy shushed him and stabbed at the control that lowered the glass.

'Honey, I missed you Friday,' the woman said. 'Our bridge afternoon wasn't the same without you. I had to partner Jane and you know what she's like. She never –'

'I had a migraine last week,' Peggy Carlton interrupted the flow of words.

'You'll be coming next week though?' The woman peered curiously at Merryck.

'Yes, sure. Dorothy, we must go, and you're getting cold.'

'Oh, all right.' She put a hand through the open window and touched the brooch Peggy Carlton was wearing at the neck of her dress. 'Is that a new pin? I noticed it in church. Was it an anniversary gift from Bill?'

There was the briefest hesitation as Peggy turned to look at her husband, then, 'No,' she said. 'An old German lady, a schoolfriend of my mother's – someone I'd never even met – bequeathed it to me when she died. It was a great surprise. I'll tell you all about it Friday.'

The window was sliding up. The car crept forward. Mrs Carlton waved. ''Bye, Dorothy,' she called. And beside her Merryck slowly released the breath he'd been holding.

He said, his voice tight, 'That sounds a fascinating story, Mrs Carlton. You never met this old lady, and she left you that beautiful brooch?'

Peggy Carlton turned to him. 'Yes, it was odd. As I said, my mother was at school with her, though they hadn't seen each other since I don't know when. But they kept in touch with occasional mail, and when Mom died I took up the correspondence. Poor Frau Schmidt. I think we'd only exchanged a couple of letters when she died.'

'Then that lovely brooch suddenly shot through your letter-box?' Merryck said, hoping they wouldn't think him excessively importunate.

'Yes,' Mrs Carlton seemed to have lost interest.

'Not exactly, dear. It wasn't quite as simple as that,' Bill Carlton corrected her.

'Oh no. Actually, Hugh, the brooch was sent to Lotte,' Peggy Carlton explained. 'I'd told Frau Schmidt Lotte was married to a Pierre Legros and was living in Neuilly. She must have looked up the address in the phone book or something.'

'I think she was afraid of the US Customs,' Bill Carlton said. 'You know what kind of a reputation they've got overseas,' he added, laughing. 'Anyway, inside Lotte's envelope the packet was addressed to Peggy here, with a request to deliver it by hand when possible. Luckily a colleague of Pierre's was coming to New York, and he was able to bring it to us.'

'I've only had it a few days,' Peggy said, and changed the subject as they turned into the driveway. 'Ah, that's Steve's automobile. Good. He can have brunch with us.'

Damn Steve Ross, Merryck thought fiercely. Damn them all, he was inclined to add. But he knew he was really swearing at himself. He had been convinced that the packet Father Anselm had sent to Lotte would lead him to Otto Krasner, and he'd been wrong. Bill Carlton was what he seemed to be, a pillar of the community, and no hasty substitute for Peggy's husband. True, there was a connection between Frau Schmidt and the Carltons, but it was very slender, and useless as far as he was concerned. Krasner was as distant as ever.

Ten

It was about nine o'clock when Martha Carlton dropped Merryck off at his hotel, Sunday evening in New York but already two o'clock the next morning in London. Once back in his room Merryck hesitated, considering. He needed to speak to Colin Grenley, but Grenley would hardly relish being woken in the small hours. However, Grenley had said his special number would be manned day and night, and he could leave a message. He sat down on the bed and dialled.

The conversation was almost a replica of the last one. The same girl's voice said evenly, 'Mr Grenley's office.' It made no comment on the hour. Again, Merryck identified himself, and again the voice said, 'Where are you, Mr Merryck? We've been waiting for you to phone.'

'In New York,' Merryck replied. 'Please ask Mr Grenley to call me back when he wakes in the morning.' He gave the number.

'All right, Mr Merryck. But you're sure you don't want me to get in touch with Colin now?'

'There's absolutely no need. It's not urgent. The morning will be fine.'

Merryck hung up. There was certainly no urgency, he thought; his news would be almost entirely negative. Depressed and disgruntled, he tried the television set, but in spite of the multiplicity of channels could find nothing to hold his interest. He paced up and down his room for a while, and lowered the level in a bottle of whisky. Finally, his sense of failure heavy in him, he took some hotel letterhead, and made three or four pages of notes in preparation for his talk with Grenley. Then he undressed and went to bed. Surprisingly, he slept.

The phone woke him. Blearily he looked at his watch. Half past three. The hotel operator said, 'I'm very sorry, sir, but I've a transatlantic call for you. The caller insists it's important.'

'That's all right,' said Merryck quickly, now fully alert. 'I should have told you I was expecting it.' Then, 'Colin –'

'Hello, Hugh. You asked to be called first thing. I gather you got to New York safely. What's the score? You said you were making progress.'

'Yes I know, Colin. I hoped I was. Unfortunately since then I've come to a dead end.'

'Tell me.'

Merryck grabbed his notes. He was, of course, talking on an open line, so he gave a carefully worded and somewhat expurgated account of his enquiries. He avoided any mention of Klaus Gerhardt's death, for example, but he told Grenley about Father Anselm and the package, his meeting with Lotte Legros and his weekend with the Carltons. He never suggested that he'd believed himself about to contact Otto Krasner – he saw no reason to parade his stupidity – but merely implied that he'd had hopes of a lead from Frau Schmidt's schoolfriend.

'Mrs Carlton herself was no use to us, and I doubt if her mother would have been any better, even if she was still alive. Her contact with Frau Schmidt was pretty tenuous, as far as I can see. But I couldn't know that when I decided to come over here,' Merryck concluded, a little defensively.

'No, I appreciate that,' Grenley said. 'You're sure about Mrs Carlton – that she didn't know any more than she was prepared to tell you, I mean?'

'Yes. Quite sure,' Merryck spoke without hesitation. 'I'm sorry, Colin, but as I said, Frau Schmidt's old schoolfriend's turned out a complete loss.'

There was silence at the other end of the line, and Merryck wondered if Grenley was trying to find the right words with which to sack him. Polite words they would be, and kind.

Grenley was a considerate chap. But the end result would be the same.

Merryck said, 'There's one other thing, Colin. I don't think I'm alone in this.'

'Not alone? What on earth do you mean?'

'Well, it looks as if there are at least a couple of people ahead of me – on the same track, you could say.'

'I see,' said Grenley. There was another pause, then suddenly, 'A couple, did you say?'

'Yes?'

'D'you know who?'

It was Merryck's turn to hesitate. 'Well,' he said slowly. 'It's hard to explain. But one lot could be the – the Company, and the other lot may be our chums from over the wall.'

'Okay. I'm with you,' said Grenley at once. 'So what are you planning to do next, Hugh?'

Surprised, Merryck seized on the obvious reprieve. The trouble was that he had little idea what to suggest. The trail had gone cold and he'd have to start again. With the police looking for Gerhardt's murderer the thought of returning to Bonn gave him no joy. But Berlin was a possibility, though not particularly promising. Still, he'd rather neglected Herr Schmidt's family, some of whom had attended Martha's funeral.

Sounding as positive as he could, he said, 'Come back to Europe and try a different tack.'

'Fine. But come via London and we'll discuss the whole thing. You can fill me in on all the details. You never know, I might have a bright idea.'

'Fair enough. I'll be there tomorrow.'

'Call the usual number when you arrive. I'll leave a message. Right? See you then, Hugh.'

'Okay.'

The line went dead before Merryck had time to say goodbye, but he had no complaints. He was still in business in spite of the lack of results, and he blessed Grenley for his forbearance. But what he needed now, he thought grimly, was a stroke of luck.

It came that Monday morning, though at first it was scarcely recognizable.

After breakfast, Merryck arranged his return flight to London, packed, left his luggage in the hotel checkroom and paid his bill. The first seat he'd been able to obtain was on an aircraft that didn't leave Kennedy until the evening, so he found himself at a loose end. He decided to spend the morning at the Metropolitan Museum, and was on his way out of the hotel when he noticed the florist's.

He stopped in his tracks. True, he'd taken Mrs Carlton a gift of chocolates, but the family had been very kind to him and it would be a pleasant gesture, he thought, to send flowers as well. Retracing his steps, he went into the shop and gave the order. It occurred to him that Martha might like some roses and he was tempted, but he finally rejected the idea. He would telephone her in the course of the afternoon, tell her his business was completed and say goodbye. There was no point in making more of their brief relationship.

He caught a cab up Fifth Avenue to the Museum, passed an enjoyable morning and, after lunch at a Schraft's, returned to the hotel. He was sorry to be leaving New York – the exhilarating city fascinated him – and he wished he had an excuse to stay longer. But there was no possible reason to prolong his visit, and Grenley was expecting him in London.

He was crossing the lobby when he heard someone calling his name. It was the salesgirl from the florist's, a tall, attractive blonde, to whom he'd earlier given his order. Slightly breathless, she caught up with him.

'Mr Merryck, sir, am I ever glad to see you!'

Merryck grinned. 'That's very nice – but why?'

'It's those flowers you ordered. I tried, but I couldn't

have them delivered. You must have given me the wrong address.'

'I most certainly did not. Are you sure the driver went to the right house?'

'Yes, sir!' The blonde nodded emphatically. 'Sure I'm sure. It's my first day in the shop, and I don't want any mistakes. The driver was in when our branch called to say they couldn't make the delivery, and I spoke to him myself. He went to 9, Acacia Drive, but it's the home of a Mr and Mrs Garland. According to the maid, they've lived there for the last four years. She'd never heard of anyone called Carlton.'

Merryck swallowed hard. He felt suddenly cold. There had to be a mistake; there had to be. But it wasn't his. He remembered Martha saying, 'Welcome to Acacia Drive', and he'd seen the name several times on the street sign at the end of the road. He could visualize the number 'Nine' in wrought-iron script over the front door. There was no question but that he'd spent the weekend at 9, Acacia Drive – with Martha Carlton and her family.

'Are you sure you've got the name right?' the blonde asked helpfully. 'I did check, and there's no Carlton in the phone book, not in Westchester County.'

Merryck thought for a moment. 'No, I'm not so sure,' he said. 'In fact, you're probably right. I did get it wrong. I'm very grateful. Many thanks.'

The blonde stared at him doubtfully. 'But what about the order, if I can't fill it?'

'Look, it's been paid for. Let's say you hang on to the flowers for the moment, and I'll let you know. All right?'

'Okay, if that's the way you want it, Mr Merryck.'

'I do. Thanks,' Merryck said again. He left her standing and frowning after him, aware that more had gone wrong than the delivery of some flowers. Certainly Merryck wasn't concerned with them. He went directly to the reception desk, said his plans had changed and was reallocated the room he'd had for the previous nights. Upstairs, his bag and briefcase brought up from the checkroom by a bell boy, he unpacked and settled down at the telephone.

First he cancelled his seat on the London flight. Then, with the help of the hotel operator, he obtained a selection of telephone numbers – for a Garland, a Ross and two Bensons, all in the area of the 'Carltons'' home – and confirmed that there was no Carlton in the relevant books. He dialled the Garland number.

'The Garland residence.' It was an unfamiliar voice, possibly that of the daily help Martha had mentioned.

'Is Mrs Garland there?'

'No, sir. She's gone to do some marketing, but she'll be home any minute now.'

'Thanks. I'll call again.'

'Who –'

But Merryck had cut the connection. Next he spoke to Mrs Ross. Her husband was called Harry, her son was John, and she knew of no Steve Ross. This time Merryck apologized. A further call established that the two Benson families were related, but not to any Agnes or Perry. Finally, he tried the Garland number again.

'Hello.' It was a different voice. Peggy Carlton?

'Peggy?' he said, attempting to disguise his English accent.

'Yes. Who is that?' Merryck said nothing and she repeated, 'Who's calling, please?'

Gently Merryck put down his receiver. He was no longer in any doubt, and he'd been tempted to say 'Hugh Merryck' and await her response, but it was better to keep them guessing. She might think it was a wrong number, the name a coincidence. And he hadn't yet decided how he was going to handle the situation.

He suddenly realized he was coldly, furiously angry and he knew what he would have liked to do. Storm into No. 9, Acacia Drive and go quietly berserk, put the fear of God into all of them. But it wasn't possible. He'd never find Otto Krasner that way. But he hated being played for a sucker, and he swore aloud, long and fluently – he hadn't been a soldier for nothing and his vocabulary was wide – and even though there was no one to hear his outburst, it helped to release his pent-up emotions.

Then he set himself to think. The priest hadn't lied. He had sent Martha Schmidt's package to Lotte Legros, as Martha had asked. Lotte, disturbed by the visit of an Englishman making enquiries about Frau Schmidt, had alerted her sister. She in turn must have alerted – who? It must have been the CIA. Only the Agency had the facilities to do such a professional job so quickly and efficiently. The plan had been to provide a phoney background for the two girls in order to allay the prying foreigner's suspicions. And they'd damned near succeeded, Merryck thought savagely.

With a few deft touches – a mixture of family photographs, an oil painting of Martha and Lotte as children, some monogrammed towels in the guest bathroom – the Garland household had been transformed into the Carlton home. Friends and neighbours had been provided, Steve Ross and the Bensons, and a spurious son who had to be adopted because his colouring was all wrong. He was prepared to bet the whole cast were members of the CIA, with their wives co-opted for the occasion. No wonder they were so much at ease with each other, and could talk so happily of parties and visits and mutual acquaintances.

They'd played their parts well. He gave them best there. Even Martha, in a sense the odd one out, had been perfectly coached. His mouth twisted bitterly as he thought of her. He had liked Martha Carlton, more than liked perhaps. If he were honest about it, he'd admit to being very attracted by her. Well, he'd not be taken in again, but if the occasion arose he wouldn't hesitate to use her.

His thoughts, which had gone off at a tangent, returned to the weekend he'd just spent, courtesy of the United States Government. It had been a good job, but a risky one. So much could have gone wrong, almost had gone wrong when he'd insisted on going to church, but even there Bill and

Peggy had been lucky. By arriving late for the service and hurrying away afterwards they'd managed to avoid meeting most of their real neighbours. What was more, their parson's warm greeting had lulled his suspicions to such an extent that he'd accepted the – in retrospect perhaps too slick – explanation of the package and its contents. Peggy must have thought quickly to use the excuse of that woman's query to tell the story; presumably she'd worn the brooch in readiness for a cue from some other member of the 'family' later in the day.

Merryck gritted his teeth as he recalled the details. Nevertheless, reviewing the past had helped him to decide what to do. He must play it very cool. He sat down and wrote a thank-you note to Mrs Carlton, saying how much he'd enjoyed the weekend, and how much he hoped to meet them again since it now seemed he would be staying in New York for some days. As a postscript he added that he hoped she'd received the flowers he'd sent.

Then he phoned De Gruchy and Grand, to be told that Miss Martha Carlton had already left for the day. Martha had given him such a run-around that he was almost surprised to find her home number listed quite openly in the Manhattan book. She answered the call herself. Merryck repeated much of what he'd said in his note to her 'mother', and asked her to have dinner with him towards the end of the week.

'My bit of business has turned out to be more complicated than I expected,' he said, grinning at the irony of his remark, 'but I hope I'll have made some progress by next Thursday. If you could keep that evening for me, I'd be overjoyed.'

'Thursday?'

'Yes. I'm sorry it's so far ahead.'

'That's – that's okay, Hugh. I'd like that. What time?'

'May I give you a call, let you know?'

'Yes. Sure.'

But she didn't sound any too sure, and Merryck said goodbye, well satisfied. He wanted Martha to be worried, doubtful about his intentions. He wanted the Garlands and Steve Ross and Ken whatever-his-name-was to begin to suspect that their weekend conspiracy had been a waste of time and money and effort. He wanted the next move to come from the CIA.

Eleven

Merryck woke early the next morning, and decided to breakfast downstairs. He was ready to leave his room at about eight o'clock, and had just put down the phone after leaving a vaguely-worded message with Grenley's girl in London that something had come up and he'd postponed his departure from New York for a few days, when it rang again. He said, 'Hello,' and when no one answered repeated himself. Still there was no response. 'Hello,' he said for the third time. 'Who's that? Who do you want?'

For a moment the open line sang, then there was a loud click and a voice said, 'This is the hotel operator. I'm sorry sir. That was an outside call, but the caller cleared.'

'You've no idea who it was? It wasn't from overseas? I've just been talking to London.'

'No, Mr Merryck. It was just a man who asked for you, but —'

'Yes?'

'I was on duty on Saturday evening, sir, and I think the same man called then. There was no answer from your room, so I checked with reception and told the caller you were away for the weekend, but your room was being held.'

'I see,' said Merryck. 'Right. Thanks. If he rings again, I'll be in the coffee shop.'

'Okay, sir.'

But Merryck was able to enjoy his breakfast without interruption, leafing idly through the *New York Times*, and considering the position. The phone calls were almost certainly efforts to check up on him, but if the CIA didn't know where he'd been for the weekend and what he was up to, they damn well ought to. Why the hell they should feel it necessary to confirm his whereabouts in this clumsy fashion was beyond imagining. And if it wasn't the CIA, who was it?

Shelving the problem, Merryck strolled through the lobby to the elevators. On his way he noticed that a batch of foreign newspapers had now appeared on the news-stand including *Die Welt* and *Frankfurter Allgemeine Zeitung*. He bought a copy of each and, back in his room, searched carefully through them. But either there was no more news of Klaus Gerhardt's murder or, if there was, it had appeared over the weekend and he'd missed it. He gave a grunt of annoyance. The day had begun in a most frustrating fashion. He could only hope it would improve.

Not knowing how long he would be in New York, Merryck decided to make the most of his time and do a little sight-seeing. He consulted the bell captain, and caught a bus to the Battery at the southern tip of Manhattan, where it was cold and windy, with a stiff breeze coming off the East River. Here, shivering, he duly saluted the Statue of Liberty, watched the Staten Island Ferry starting its trip across New York Bay and thought about his next move. Then, at a brisk pace to keep himself warm, he set off past the Bowling Green up Broadway – here far removed from the lights of theatre-land – past Wall Street and the canyons of the financial district towards Greenwich Village. Some while before he reached Canal Street, he realized he was being followed.

There were two of them. He spotted the one in the brown duffel coat first and, several minutes later, the one in the blue raincoat. They were both broad and strongly built but, at the distance they kept, it was impossible to note anything else distinctive about them.

Merryck was amused. He watched them watching him with a sardonic satisfaction, and made no attempt to lose them. If the CIA wanted to follow him around, they were more than welcome. It certainly wouldn't get them very far.

By now it was noon, and he was beginning to feel hungry. He chose a likely-looking bar and went inside. There were three or four men on stools at the counter and a couple in an alcove. Merryck chose a seat in the window, from where through the dark-coloured glass he could keep an eye on the street.

He knew he'd been seen coming into the bar, and he was curious about what his tails would do. He wasn't long left in doubt. The man in the duffel coat walked past the window without a glance in Merryck's direction, and the other watcher came into the bar, sat himself up at the counter and asked for a beer.

Merryck finished his drink and had a light lunch. The man had ordered a sandwich. Merryck paid his bill. The man did the same. Merryck went to the washroom at the far end of the bar. The man followed him. Merryck left the bar and continued walking northwards up Broadway. The man stayed some twenty yards behind him. There was no sign of his duffel-coated companion.

Merryck was getting bored. What had at first seemed a joke was becoming an irritant. Either the Agency considered him too much of a fool to spot their blatant tailing, or they didn't care if he did spot it. Either explanation seemed somewhat insulting. Clearly they deserved a lesson.

Merryck stopped at a kerb and glanced to his left as if to check on the traffic before crossing the road. From the corner of his eye he caught a glimpse of a blue raincoat, but 'duffel coat' was still nowhere to be seen. Merryck dodged across the road, took the first turning he came to, sprinted down a rather mean street and into a narrow alley. He slipped into a doorway and waited.

A black and white cat lost interest in an overturned garbage can, and came to rub himself against Merryck's legs. Then there was a sound of hurrying footsteps. 'Blue raincoat' went past, and Merryck sprang out of his hiding-place.

'Hi there!' he shouted.

The man whipped round but Merryck was already on him, pushing him violently against a wall so that his head banged back against the dirty bricks. The man swore, and Merryck almost released him. The man had sworn in German.

But at once he spoke in English. 'What is it? What do you want? Money? You are welcome to what I have.'

Merryck overcame his surprise; he'd been certain his tails were CIA. 'All I want is to know why you've been following me this morning – mein Herr,' he said fiercely. 'Tell –'

'Following you? No, no, you are wrong. I am a tourist. I have been looking at the sights of New York.'

'You're German, *nicht wahr*? From the East?'

'German, yes. But from the Federal Republic. You can see my passport if you doubt me.'

Merryck laughed without mirth. 'Your passport? What would that mean? You bought it, or your government forged it. Are you working for your government? Or are you private enterprise?'

'Bitte sprechen Sie langsamer. I don't understand. What is this private enterprise?'

'Don't give me that!' Merryck shook him so that his head hit the wall again. The man offered no resistance. He was smaller than Merryck and appeared to shrink from him, his glance darting from side to side as if seeking a means of escape. But Merryck wasn't taken in by this show of timidity. He kept his eyes firmly fixed on the man in front of him, expecting a sudden move.

'Answer me!'

As he spoke Merryck sensed a movement behind him. At the same time his prisoner's gaze fixed itself on a point beyond Merryck's shoulder, and almost imperceptibly he nodded. But this was an old trick and Merryck, feeling the cat press against his leg again, blamed the animal and paid no attention.

Then the cat leapt away. Merryck felt a rush of air and swung round hastily. The other watcher, the man in the duffel coat, was there, arm upraised, a wicked-looking cosh in his hand, ready to strike. The cosh began its downward path and Merryck acted fast and instinctively. Feinting sideways, he kicked upwards and, as the toe of his shoe made contact with his attacker's wrist, the man screamed and dropped the cosh. In those split seconds Merryck recognized him. He was the East German 'diplomat' who, just over a week ago, had been engaged in tailing Merryck in Bonn.

The German's face was the last thing Merryck saw before he plunged forward into nothingness. He had been quick, but not quick enough. To guard against the immediate threat he had been forced to turn his back on the man he himself had been threatening and, for this neglect, had paid the price. He had been struck neatly and efficiently behind the ear.

The blow was well-judged. Merryck came to almost as soon as he hit the ground, but he felt no wish to get up. It was as if he were temporarily paralysed. He lay, fighting the nausea that rose in his throat. Above him there was a mutter of German, a shout, running footsteps. A shoe kicked his head. Then more footsteps, another cry, and someone knelt beside him. Merryck opened his eyes carefully.

An unfamiliar face was looking down at him. An unfamiliar voice, but with a reassuring American accent, was saying, 'Jeez! Are you okay? I thought for a minute there –'

'I'm all right,' Merryck said. 'And thanks. If you'd not come along I might have been far from okay. I wasn't expecting to be mugged in broad daylight.'

'Mugged?' For a moment the American seemed oddly nonplussed. Then, 'Oh, sure,' he said. 'It can happen any time in this city. Here, what about getting you up off the ground?'

As Merryck staggered to his feet the world revolved and he leaned against his companion – to be thrust away slightly, but supported. He let himself sag, pretending he hadn't felt the hard outline under the American's coat, and studied his rescuer more closely.

The American was in his late thirties. His body was

113

compact and well-muscled. His face was quite pleasant, apart from an over-firm jaw and mouth, but singularly lacking in expression. All in all, he didn't look the type to interfere unasked in someone else's quarrel, or go out of his way to play the good Samaritan. And he carried a gun.

'The police,' said Merryck. 'Should we –'

'Sure, if you like,' the man said. 'But there's not much point. The muggers have gone. Did they take anything?'

'No, I don't think so,' Merryck said. 'I'm sure you're right. But I wonder if you'd help me find a cab. If it's not asking too much.'

'Of course.' The man bent and picked up the cosh the German had dropped when Merryck kicked him, and was about to slip it in his pocket.

Merryck held out his hand. 'Can I have that? A memento, you know, for when I get back to England. It'll back up my story when I tell my friends about this fracas. Quite an adventure, it's been.'

The American hesitated. But, with no choice, he gave Merryck the cosh, and together they walked slowly down the alley. Merryck introduced himself, adding that he was in New York partly on business, partly on pleasure. 'And you?' he said.

'John Adamson. I live here, in the city.'

'You mean you're a genuine New Yorker. You were born here?'

'No,' said Adamson shortly. To Merryck, it seemed a rather churlish monosyllabic reply to an innocuous question, but Adamason quickly added, 'I was born and raised in upstate New York, a small town called Willowdale. I doubt if you'll have heard of it.'

He was right. Merryck hadn't heard of it. But it gave him the opening he'd been angling for. He swung round as if in pleased surprise. 'Then you know Steve Ross?'

Adamson didn't falter. His face remained expressionless and his voice was without emotion as he said, 'No, I don't think I know any Steve Ross.' But the sudden tightening of his jawline betrayed him and that was enough for Merryck, who hadn't expected more.

'That's funny,' Merryck said. 'I met this chap – Steve Ross – last weekend, and I could have sworn he said he came from Willowdale. He was about your age, and if Willowdale's really a small town –'

Adamson made no reply. He was busy flagging down a cab. When one drew up at the kerb he helped Merryck in, and got in beside him. 'Where to, Mr Merryck?'

Merryck gave him the name of his hotel, and added, 'But – please. I'm all right now. I don't want to take you out of your way.'

'That's okay. I'm going uptown, and I'll be glad of a ride.'

Merryck didn't argue. If the CIA man wanted to see him safely back to his hotel it was fine by him. He didn't believe the Germans would have done him any further harm, even if Adamson hadn't arrived on the scene. They'd been following him all the morning without attempting to accost him, and had only attacked him in self-defence. Nevertheless, he was grateful to Adamson.

He sat back in the cab and shut his eyes. His head hurt. Damn those Germans! It was reasonable enough for the CIA to keep an eye on him. He'd expected it, which was why he'd jumped to the conclusion that his two watchers were from the Agency. But why on earth should the East Germans be following him at such trouble and expense? He thought he'd lost 'duffel coat' in Bonn, but the man must have tailed him to Paris and then on to New York. It was a major operation. Why?

Frau Schneider had said there were two self-styled 'cousins' also interested in Martha Schmidt. By now there was no doubt in Merryck's mind. One represented the CIA and the other the GDR intelligence or security services – in effect, the Governments of the United States and of the Democratic Republic. And he himself was very much the odd man out – or in the middle. It was an invidious position, Merryck thought, remembering Klaus Gerhardt, and one he didn't much appreciate.

Twelve

The day after the incident with the two East Germans was largely uneventful; even the bruise behind Merryck's ear was fading. Once, when he came out of Schwartz's, where he'd been buying presents for his brother's children, he thought he caught a glimpse of 'duffel coat', but he wasn't sure. And, though he kept his eyes open, he saw no sign of 'blue raincoat' or of John Adamson. Possibly he had new tails, but they weren't obvious, and Merryck made no effort to identify or avoid them.

In the evening he went to a Broadway theatre, where one of the latest musicals cheered him considerably. He was beginning to wonder if his tactics would pay off. He had hoped – assumed, even – that by now the CIA would have taken some positive action, but they seemed content to do no more than watch him, if indeed they were still doing that. There was a limit to how long he could continue to enjoy New York at the FCO's expense; he couldn't expect the vague message he'd left with London yesterday to hold Grenley indefinitely. If the CIA didn't act soon, he'd have to precipitate some action himself.

Humming the hit number from the show he'd just seen, Merryck strode along the hotel corridor to his room. His mind half on the song and half on his current problems, he was fitting his key into the lock before he noticed the light shining under his door. At once he was on the alert. He was sure he'd put out all the lights before he left, and it was unlikely that a maid had been in the room since. Therefore, he'd had an unexpected visitor. Keeping well to the side of the frame, he suddenly flung the door back on its hinges.

'Hi, Hugh. I thought you'd never come.'

Momentarily Merryck clenched his teeth. He slid cautiously into the open doorway. Martha Carlton, wearing a blue wool dress that matched her eyes, was sitting in an armchair. She had been watching a television programme and looked completely at ease, as if the room were hers rather than Merryck's. She gave him a wide smile.

Merryck grinned in return, pretending he'd not been disconcerted. 'If I'd known you were here nothing would have kept me away,' he said, with some truth. Then he shut the door and advanced into the room. 'Incidentally, how did you get in? Did you pick the lock?'

Martha switched off the TV set. 'Oh no. One of the housekeepers let me in with her pass key. I told her you were expecting me.'

On the surface, this seemed an unlikely explanation, but Merryck didn't question its veracity. It was irrelevant. What was important was Martha's reason for visiting him in this way. He couldn't believe she'd come of her own accord, and for his sake. He regarded her speculatively, smiling.

'Delighted as I am to see you,' he said, 'I must admit to some curiosity. Why?'

'You sound very English,' Martha said. Her expression changed. 'Why am I here?' Her smile became rueful. 'I'm here, Hugh, because I want to apologize to you, to tell you –'

'Apologize!' Merryck perched on the end of the bed. 'My dear Martha, what are you talking about?'

'You know darn well what I'm talking about. Don't play games!' For a second her temper flared, then she had it under control. 'That sham of a weekend with my so-called family, of course. Oh, I don't blame you for being angry about it, Hugh. It was a crazy thing to try on. But I hoped that once you were convinced you were on the wrong track you'd go away and my father would be safe. He's a good, kind man and he's got a heart condition. Why can't you leave him alone, let him die in peace? Is that too much to ask? He's never done you English any harm.'

'And I don't intend him any harm either. Martha, you

must believe me.' Sliding off the bed, Merryck pulled up the dressing-table stool and sat directly before her so that their knees were almost touching. 'What do you say we try to be honest with each other – for a change?'

Martha stared directly into Merryck's eyes. 'Right,' she said. 'Right. Then what do you want of my father?'

'Your father – Otto Krasner?'

'No!' Martha was vehement. 'No, not Krasner! His name's Carlton – Otto Carlton – and it has been for twenty-five years. What came before is past history. It's not important any more.'

'Martha, unfortunately it is, extremely important. Which is why I want to talk to your father – why I've got to talk to him. But that's all I want, just a chance to talk. I mean him no harm, I swear it.'

Martha turned her head away and sighed. 'Why should I believe you?' And when Merryck said nothing, she added, 'Suppose I said it was impossible. You can't meet him. He's not even living in the USA. What would you say then?'

There was a lot he might say, Merryck thought sardonically, but most of it was better left unsaid. He didn't trust Martha's new approach. He didn't really trust Martha at all, much as he would like to. Nevertheless, he must play along with her. It was just possible he might be allowed to meet Krasner if he could convince her – and through her the CIA – that such a meeting would be best for Krasner in the long run.

He said carefully, 'I know a great deal about your father, Martha. If I wished him ill I could easily make what I know public. Even the information that he's still alive would cause worldwide interest. The CIA could try to spirit him away to some new secret hide-out, but even they couldn't give him another fresh start, another new persona, not at this stage of his life. They might try, but I doubt if he'd be happy.'

Martha pushed back her chair and stood up, looking down at him. 'Is that meant to be what it sounds like, Hugh Merryck? A threat? You're prepared to bully an old, sick man, cause him great sadness, put his life in danger maybe – and make Lotte and me sick with the worry of it all? And for what? Tell me why!' Martha's voice trembled with her emotion. Her eyes were blazing, and Merryck could see the whiteness of her knuckles as she clasped her hands in front of her, digging the nails into her palms.

She wasn't acting – not at the moment. Merryck was certain of that. Only a superb, trained actress could give such a performance. Merryck would have liked to reach up his hands, unclench her fists, touch her face, take her into his arms and kiss away her anger and her fears. Then he remembered Steve Ross.

He said, 'Martha, I'm not threatening your father, or anyone connected with him. All I'm doing is stating facts. Listen. When Johann Meissener and your father tried to escape to the West twenty-five years ago, they were be- trayed. Someone knew of their plan and told the authorities. One man was suspected of the betrayal. He's dead now, but his family believe your father might be able to clear his name.'

'But if he's dead what does his name matter?'

'It matters to his family. Very much. It's terribly impor- tant to them.'

'Not as important as my father's safety.'

'Martha, this is going to sound like another threat. But if I go back to England and say I've failed to talk to Otto Krasner, the family – the suspected man's family – are going to put on the pressure. You must believe me when I say they've got a lot of clout – political and social. So far they've been happy to keep the matter quiet and private, but there are reasons why they may not be prepared to go on taking that sort of view. If you refuse to co-operate, they could make life very unpleasant for your father and really endanger him.'

'Oh God! Why did Aunt Martha have to lose that letter?' Martha said sadly. 'Things have been grim ever since. We've known about Dad for three years. He told us – Lotte and me – when Mom died. At the time it didn't seem to matter much.

But now we're scared witless. Dad tries to make light of it, but Steve Ross doesn't. He knows that Dad's enemies from the old days in East Germany'll never forget, and they don't play games.'

Merryck noted the reference to the GDR, but made no comment. Instead he said, 'So Steve Ross is in charge of the operation.' Then he asked gently, 'Did he tell you to come here tonight?'

Martha stared at him. 'Steve's responsible for Dad's safety, and of course I help. I'd do anything for Dad – anything.'

She hadn't given a direct answer to his question about Ross, Merryck noticed, but he didn't press the point. It hardly mattered. He got to his feet and held out both hands to her. 'Martha, trust me. Please. Get in touch with your father and tell him what I've told you. I think he'll be willing to see me. I hope he will. If he does, I promise I'll do my utmost to make sure he's not bothered again.'

Martha gave him a long, doubting look. Then she seemed to relax. She shrugged and smiled. 'All right, Hugh. I'll trust you. I guess I don't have much choice, do I? First thing in the morning I'll try and fix something. It's much too late now.' She had disregarded the hands Merryck held out to her, but as she spoke she came close to him and slipped her arms around his neck. 'You won't let me down, will you?' she said, her lips almost brushing his.

'I'll do my very best not to,' Merryck repeated in a murmur, pulling her to him. And as his mouth came down hard on hers, he found it difficult to believe that she was still acting under orders – Ross's orders, the Agency's orders.

In the morning when Merryck came out of the shower, Martha was lying back against the pillows, hair slightly dishevelled, blue eyes wide and smiling, looking up at him. He thought how beautiful she was and, as the sheet slipped below her breasts and he felt himself harden, how much he desired her. But there was more to it than that – some kind of affinity between them that he sensed, or imagined he sensed. It was a long time since any girl had got to him like this.

Cutting short the sentiment, telling himself not to be a fool, Merryck said, 'You won't forget, will you, Martha? About your father, I mean.'

'No, Hugh, I won't forget. I'll call you around noon. Will you be here?'

'I'll be here,' said Merryck. 'I'll be waiting.' Then, casually, 'Where is your father, if he's not in Westchester?'

Martha hesitated. 'Don't ask me that, Hugh – not yet. I'm not sure I should tell you till I've – I've talked to him.' She slipped out of bed quickly and made for the bathroom. 'You finished in there?'

'Yes. Go ahead. Shall I order up some breakfast? Double helpings for one?'

She grinned in reply. 'No. I must hurry or I'll be late. I'll grab a coffee at the office, thanks.'

In the event they went downstairs together, Martha bound for her work, Merryck for the Coffee Shop. They had spoken no words of endearment since they woke that morning but, before they left the room, Martha had reached up and kissed him gently on the cheek. 'Thank you,' she said quietly.

It was just after noon when the phone rang in Merryck's room. Martha sounded breathless, tense perhaps. 'I'm calling from the office,' she said at once. 'I can't talk for long, but it's all fixed. He agrees. He'll talk to you and answer your questions. But he says I should – should warn you, Hugh. He thinks he knows what you're getting at, and he may not be able to help you.'

Merryck breathed a silent sigh of relief. 'Fair enough. I'll take the risk. If I can just have a chat with him, that's all I want. Thanks a lot, Martha. Where and when?'

Martha said, 'Well, I've arranged to take a day's vacation tomorrow. We can fly up in the morning.'

122

'Fly? Tomorrow? Where to?' Merryck had expected at least a minimum of delay and prevarication.

'Toronto, Ontario. I told you Dad wasn't in the United States. And why not fly? We could drive, but it's quite a way and the weather's not to be trusted this time of year. We'd be going through the snow belt upstate and there could still be a heavy fall. It'll be better to rent a car at Toronto airport. Look, I'll make all the reservations and call you again later, Hugh.'

'Martha, why not have dinner with me tonight? We can check the arrangements then.'

'I may have to work late if I'm to be off tomorrow.' She had spoken without hesitation and the excuse sounded genuine.

Merryck pressed her. 'I don't mind how late I eat.'

'Okay, but I've a better idea. Come along to my apartment about nine and I'll cook you a steak.'

'And we could leave together for the airport in the morning? That would be the best idea of all.'

Martha seemed to hesitate, then she laughed. 'It had occurred to me too,' she said.

And why not, he asked himself a little cynically as he put down the receiver a moment or two later, why not mix business with pleasure? He wished he knew how Martha really felt about him. Probably much as he did about her, he supposed. He had enough experience of women to know she had enjoyed the previous night. That, at least, hadn't been pretence, but her manner on the phone just now had been a little odd – reserved, constrained, perhaps? She seemed to have organized the interview with Krasner as she'd promised, but still . . .

Momentarily exasperated at his inability to reconcile his growing feeling for Martha with the role she was undoubtedly playing, Merryck looked at his watch. It was still early in London, but he expected to be busy later in the day. He picked up the phone again and dialled. The same girl answered Grenley's number, and Merryck wondered if she ever slept.

'I expect to be going to Canada tomorrow,' he said abruptly as soon as he'd given his name.

'Canada? Where?'

'I'm not sure yet, but I'm flying in to Toronto. I don't know how long I'll be there, but I should have some news afterwards.'

'Right. I'll pass that on. Is that all?'

'For the moment, yes. Anything your end?'

'No. Just take care, Mr Merryck, and if you're going up to Canada buy yourself a warm coat. It'll probably be freezing there.'

The line went dead and Merryck grinned. The voice was human after all. And its advice was good. He would buy himself a coat – and he would take good care.

In the hotel Coffee Shop again, munching a club sandwich for lunch and sipping a beer, Merryck tried to make plans. If Martha was to be believed – and there was no obvious reason why she should lie about this – it was Krasner's one-time fellow-countrymen, the East Germans, who offered the main threat to his security and peace of mind, if not to his very life. And Merryck had no wish to lead Krasner's enemies to him, even unintentionally.

Last weekend, perhaps stupidly, he had failed to consider the possibility of being followed and had gone off to West-chester with Martha quite overtly. Luckily, no harm seemed to have resulted from his carelessness. Indeed there was no evidence they had been tailed – except of course by Steve Ross. Maybe it had been Ross's task to keep an eye out for suspicious watchers, and provide a measure of protection by running interference. This time things could be different, and Merryck himself intended to take precautions.

He left the hotel by the 59th Street entrance and walked across to Fifth Avenue, where he hailed a cab and directed it downtown to Macy's. He'd been told that, like Harrod's, Macy's could supply anything, and he felt confident he could lose himself – and any tails – in the crowded department store.

In the course of forty-five minutes meanderings, up and down escalators, through a variety of departments, he bought a padded car-coat, a knitted ski-cap and a large expansible canvas hold-all. He insisted that the coat be rolled and squashed into the hold-all with the cap, and the whole thing made into a parcel.

He spent a couple of hours in an almost empty movie house, and as a simple check he left by an inconspicuous fire exit and waited for ten minutes in the alley outside. If he had any tails, they were certainly acting with the greatest of discretion.

He returned to his hotel in the late afternoon, with time to spare. He left his purchases in his room and had a couple of drinks in the bar before going to the reception desk. Telling the clerk he was leaving early in the morning, he asked to settle his bill and, while the account was being made up, volunteered that his business in the States was now complete and that he was returning home to the UK. It was always possible that the information would be passed on to any enquirers.

Back in his room he packed. The hold-all lived up to its name. With the bulky car-coat removed it held all his possessions, including bag, briefcase, raincoat and the small presents he'd bought the day before. Only the Scotch and the bottle of wine he was taking to Martha had to stay in their carrier-bag. Merryck was well satisfied, but spent some minutes carefully smearing the new hold-all with dust he found behind the radiator.

When it was time he put on his car-coat and pulled the ski-cap over his ears. At once he looked fatter and shorter and, with the hold-all, a quite different man. He left the room key on the dressing-table, shut the door firmly behind him and walked down two storeys of fire stairs before taking the elevator to the lobby.

Looking like any other New Yorker off for the weekend

125

and hoping for good snow conditions in the Adirondacks, he let the doorman find him a cab, and murmured 'Grand Central' when he was safely inside it. The station concourse was crowded as he hurried to another exit. A second cab to the East Side Air Terminal on First Avenue and, after a pause for reconnaissance, yet another to Martha's apartment. When he arrived he could have sworn that he was clean.

Thirteen

This could be a slightly embarrassing moment, Merryck thought as, encumbered by his hold-all and the carrier bag, he rang the bell of Martha's apartment. But the sight of her in the blue wool dress that matched her eyes and brought back vivid memories of the previous night was sufficient. He dropped his baggage, kicked the door shut behind him and took her in his arms. And as he kissed her, he was conscious only of her lips, her skin, her body . . . He had to remind himself of the circumstances, warn himself that she mustn't be taken too seriously – at least not yet.

Releasing her, he said lightly, 'There's a most glorious smell and I'm ravenous. When do we eat?'

Martha laughed. She took a step back and looked at him for a moment before she spoke. Then she said, hurriedly, perhaps a little nervously, 'As soon as you're ready and we've had a drink. The bathroom's here. I'll be in the kitchen.' She added, 'The bedroom's there. You can't get lost.'

She was right, Merryck realized at once. It was hard to get lost. The apartment wasn't large, though the rooms were each of a fair size, bright and comfortably furnished. There were good modern reproductions on the walls and books everywhere, even to a shelf of paperbacks in the bathroom. As Merryck dropped his hold-all in the bedroom, he noticed some framed photographs on top of the chest of drawers. One which he had seen before, was of Lotte's wedding. Another was of a middle-aged man and woman – Otto Krasner and his late wife, Merryck assumed.

He picked up the silver frame and studied the photograph with interest. At once he saw where Martha's beauty had come from. Her mother had the same classical features, the same bone structure, the same large, deep blue eyes. But the expression was different. Though she was smiling, the woman in the photograph had a look of infinite sadness.

As for the man, his face was pleasant enough, but uninteresting, bland. It was not the face of a man who'd held power and made decisions that affected millions. The plastic surgeon, Merryck thought, had done a remarkable job. This was Otto Carlton, all-American husband and father, the kind of guy who read the sports pages first and was unconcerned with politics, an ordinary fellow who'd never set the world on fire. No one would guess that behind this façade was Otto Krasner, former East German politician, friend of the great Johann Meissener, erstwhile Communist defector.

Martha was calling. Merryck put down the photograph and hurried into the kitchen, seizing the carrier bag of liquor as he passed through the hall. He asked her about the photographs.

'Yes,' she said. 'Those are my folks.' She smiled apologetically. 'For real, this time, Hugh. Mom was first generation American. Her parents emigrated from Germany before World War Two. She was a nurse and she looked after Dad when he arrived – he was ill for quite a while – that's how they met.' Martha sounded over-talkative, almost as if anxious to forestall questions.

'She knew about your father's past?' Merryck interrupted her flow of words.

'Oh yes. She worked for – for the government.'

Over supper Martha continued to speak of her parents and Lotte and their childhood in Ontario. Clearly it had been a happy, carefree home, in spite of the secrets hidden from the daughters. Merryck marvelled that Otto Krasner had been able to adapt to such a humdrum life, running an antiquarian bookshop by day and returning to an apparently normal middle-class Canadian family each evening. Had he found it excruciatingly dull? Or had he been so thankful to be free that he'd had no regrets about the power and influence he'd abandoned. Both probably, Merryck thought with a flash of sympathy.

'. . . sold the store four years ago.' Martha was still talking, though she was smiling now and more relaxed. 'There was a boom in the book trade in Canada, and he made quite a bit out of it – both the property and the stock. We thought of moving somewhere with a better climate, Florida perhaps or the Carolinas. Lots of Canadians do when they retire. But Dad didn't want to move.'

'You've always lived in Toronto?' Merryck asked.

'Yes. We've a lovely modern house in York Mills – that's a residential area just north of the city with plenty of space and –' Martha stopped abruptly as if she'd suddenly realized she was saying too much. It was the first truly jarring note of the evening, but she recovered herself and went on immediately. 'Though we're not going there. We'll be driving up to the cottage on Lake Simcoe, about forty miles away.'

'Cottage?' Merryck said doubtfully.

Martha grinned. 'Don't worry,' she said. 'I guess it's hardly an old-fashioned summer cottage. The days of outdoor plumbing – little huts at the bottom of the back lot – they're long past, at least around Toronto. Really it's a fair-sized house, and it's fully winterized. Dad loves it. It's one of the reasons why he wouldn't leave Canada. He spends most weekends up there, when he's well enough –'

As she continued, Merryck wondered about her earlier indiscretion, if indiscretion it was. Surely there was no point in being sensitive about the details of Krasner's homes or whereabouts. After all, he'd be meeting the man tomorrow. Ross and his colleagues couldn't try a second substitution trick.

Soured by the thought of Ross, Merryck didn't protest when Martha waved away his offers to help with the clearing up, and insisted he should go and unpack what he needed for the night, while she loaded the dishwasher and made coffee. He did as he was told and went into the bedroom. His unpacking took only a moment or two and, from the sounds in the kitchen, Martha remained fully occupied.

Merryck took the opportunity to give the room a more thorough inspection than had been possible earlier. He had seen no desk in the living-room, and there was none in here, but Martha must keep bills and letters somewhere. He tried the dressing-table and found he'd guessed right first time. The top right-hand drawer was half full of neat piles of papers, carefully sorted. Martha had made it easy for him.

He rifled gently through the contents of the drawer. In a cardboard box at the bottom there were three or four letters. Merryck seized on them. A quick glance at the signature showed they were from Martha's mother – probably, from the dates, the last she had written to her daughter before she died. The printed heading at the top of each page gave an address in York Mills, Ontario.

There was a chink of coffee cups from the direction of the living-room, and Martha's voice calling. Quickly and silently Merryck replaced the letters in their box, rearranged the papers that had covered it and closed the drawer. Well content with what he'd found, he went back to the living-room – to Martha – determined not to let thoughts of Martha's father spoil their evening.

The next day, both in the cab to La Guardia and at the airport itself, Merryck kept his eyes open, but he saw no obvious signs of any watchers. The flight was uneventful and they touched down in Toronto on time. They went through Immigration and Customs and collected their rental car – a blue compact Chevrolet – and again no one seemed to take any special interest in them or their movements.

They had been given an early lunch on the aircraft, so they set off at once to join the thundering traffic on an enormous twelve-lane motorway, and before too long were leaving the built-up area on an ordinary divided highway. Snow, which had been largely cleared around the airport and the city, lay on the ground.

Merryck stared out of the window at the unfamiliar

landscape. It was flat, and white or dirty grey, except where a thaw had let areas of brown grass show through. The sky too was grey and lowering, threatening another fall before the day was out. A cold, bleak scene, and to Merryck, from the super-heated warmth of the car, strangely unreal.

But they made good time. In spite of the snow-covered fields, the road surface was bare and dry. They passed a number of exits from the highway, with signs pointing to places with familiar names – Newmarket, Bradford. For want of anything else to do Merryck began to turn occasionally and stare through the rear window. Only slowly did it become apparent that a dark grey car was keeping the same distance behind them. Ross again? A protection squad for Martha? All Merryck's suspicions were aroused, but before he'd decided on any action, Martha had turned to the right off the highway on a narrower road marked 'Gilford'. Another few minutes and they passed a sign which read, almost unbelievably, 'Welcome to Gilford. Population 108. Drive Carefully.'

Merryck had just time to glance over his shoulder and see that the grey car was still following, when Martha swung abruptly left on to a gravel track, which led past a lonely frame house of moderate size, standing in a broad snow-covered expanse that seemed to lead down to an icy lake. She brought the car to a halt in front of the house, saying in a voice both resigned and relieved, 'Here we are, Hugh. Here we are. Home.'

This might well be true, thought Merryck. It could well be the Krasner's so-called cottage. But the appearance of Steve Ross on the porch with a small automatic in his hand suggested that the welcome was unlikely to be normally hospitable. For a moment Merryck was tempted to shove hard across the bench seat in the front of car, chop Martha, unlatch her door, push her to the ground, start the engine, drive on and take his chances.

But he couldn't bring himself to risk hurting her. Besides, his curiosity was strong and there remained an outside chance that he was to meet Krasner under CIA surveillance. In any case, it was too late. Adamson had joined Ross and together they were advancing on the car. Martha sat where she was, staring straight ahead, her hands clenched on the wheel. Her job was presumably complete. She'd delivered him according to instructions. Merryck swallowed his bitterness. After all, she had warned him. She'd said she'd do anything for her father's sake.

With these somewhat contradictory thoughts in mind, Merryck climbed silently out of the car, and shivered in the cold.

'Hello, Ross – Adamson,' he said finally, his breath a white mist in the air. 'I wish I could say this was a pleasant surprise.'

'Come along in, Merryck.' Ross was unsmiling. He stood back as Merryck reached the steps up to the porch, and let him go first into the house. 'The room on your right. Adamson'll bring your bags.'

The hall was narrow and rather dark, scarcely more than a passage and with a tiled floor. Merryck turned right and went through an archway into a long, low-ceilinged room. Here the floor was wood, highly polished, with brightly coloured scatter mats, the furniture well-worn but cared for.

An old-fashioned upright piano stood in one corner, and on the piano stool sat the young man Merryck had originally met at Martha's supposed home in Westchester posing as her brother Ken Carlton. As Merryck came into the room he banged his hands down on the keys to produce a jangle of sound and swivelled on the stool to give the Englishman a cold, hard stare. At the same time came the crunch of wheels on gravel as Martha accelerated away from the house. The front door slammed. And fleetingly Merryck remembered the other car, the grey one, the one he'd thought was tailing him.

'Take your coat off slowly, Merryck. Drop it on the floor. Hands against the wall over there.' Ross gestured with his automatic. 'Spread yourself.'

Merryck was pretty sure that Ross was brandishing his gun for effect rather than actual use, and he'd have risked being wrong if he'd had anything to gain. But the earlier arguments still applied. There was no point in reacting till he'd seen how the land lay, what the CIA men had in mind. He complied with Ross's demand, and Adamson frisked him. 'He's clean, Steve.'

'Okay. Check out his coat and bag. You, Merryck, sit down. There – in the middle of that.' Ross, reversing a hard-backed chair and bestriding the seat, pointed. 'Hands on knees. Keep away from the arms. No tricks.'

Merryck sat, and found himself buried in the depths of a low, overstuffed sofa. He looked from Adamson, who had just found the German's cosh in his car-coat pocket, to Ken and then back to Ross. He smiled thinly.

'Well,' he said. 'This is a change of roles. The last time I met Adamson he was acting the good Samaritan. Then you, Ross – that weekend you were playing family friend and prospective son-in-law, while Ken here was an aspiring concert pianist. Incidentally, what's your real name, Ken? It can't possibly be Carlton.'

'Ford,' the man at the piano said sourly.

Merryck gave a nod of acknowledgement. 'So what happened? The Samaritan was disillusioned, the lover deceived, the pianist just not good enough, and –'

'Can it!'

Ken Ford was on his feet. He spat out the words. Merryck, happy to have touched a nerve, turned a wide grin on the others. Ross was controlling his temper better than Ford, but he too was furiously angry. Only Adamson, now lounging against the entrance archway, showed no emotion.

'Hold it, Ken,' Ross said. 'He's just trying to ride us.'

'Goddamn Limey son of a bitch!' Ford muttered, but he sat down again on the piano stool.

Ross said, 'Merryck, we've brought you here to ask some questions, and we intend to get straight answers. Do you understand me?'

'Sure. But couldn't you have asked me civilly? Why all this melodrama?'

Ross ignored the questions. 'Who are you working for, Merryck?'

'The Dencourt family,' Merryck said at once. 'I explained to Martha –'

'Don't give us that. We've been on to London. Okay, there were a few rumours buzzing around, but they didn't amount to a hill of beans. No one seems to have heard of you in relation to the Dencourts. You'll have to do better than that, Merryck.'

Merryck shrugged. 'I told Martha the truth, and she must have passed it on to you. The object of the exercise is to clear Francis Dencourt's name, and all I want is to talk with Otto Krasner. So what's the problem?'

'Crap!' Ross was scornful. 'Dencourt was guilty as hell. He betrayed Krasner – and Meissener. He worked for the Commies. We know it and the Brits know it though they won't admit it. And you know it too.'

'I don't *know* anything,' said Merryck. 'I'm just doing a job. But what about Krasner himself?' he demanded. 'What did he say about Dencourt twenty-five years ago? You've no idea, have you? Once he was fit enough the Agency was so keen on debriefing him on its own requirements it never bothered to ask him about Dencourt. Isn't that so? Dencourt was assumed to be guilty because he'd been screwing an East German girl.'

'One of your friends, Merryck,' Ken Ford intervened with a sneer.

'She'd be a bit long in the tooth for me by now, wouldn't she? And if you're suggesting I'm –'

Ross interrupted him. '– working for the GDR. Yes, that's precisely what we are suggesting, Merryck. You're not working officially for the Brits and you're not working for the Dencourts, not unless a whole lot of people are lying. That only leaves the –'

'Don't talk bloody nonsense!' Suddenly Merryck was

angry in his turn. 'I've got damn all to do with the GDR. Ask Adamson. He saw me being beaten up by two of them.'

'You never told me those guys were East Germans,' Adamson said.

'Why should I? You never told me you were CIA,' Merryck retorted. 'And if the Agency was keeping that close an eye on events, you should have known anyway.'

'They didn't hurt you. It could easily have been a set-up.' Adamson was indifferent.

'And how much are they paying you, Merryck?' Ross asked suddenly.

'Don't be such a fool. They're not paying me anything. I tell you I'm not working for them. What the hell do you think I'm doing for them?'

'Finding Krasner, of course. Now they've finally discovered he wasn't killed in the border crossing, they want him badly. They've got long memories, and they can guess how much harm he did them when he came over. They never like defectors – especially prominent ones – to get away with it. It might encourage others. But you know all this, Merryck – better than I do.'

'Oh, for God's sake! Look, why aren't they doing the job themselves? Why employ me? They don't know me from Adam.'

'So you say.' Now Ross was sarcastic. 'They didn't get anywhere by themselves in Bonn, and they needed someone who wasn't on any relevant files but had the right skills – just like you, Merryck.' Ross paused and then added casually, 'Incidentally, how did you get on to Lotte Legros?'

Merryck didn't hesitate. He had no wish to involve Father Anselm. 'Frau Schneider, Martha Schmidt's friend, told me about sending the packet to her.'

'That's a lie for a start, Merryck. I talked to Frau Schneider myself. She knew nothing of Frau Schmidt's relations.'

'You mean she didn't tell you about them, Ross. Too bad. She said she didn't like you much. I don't blame her. You should have paid more attention to her, and less to the postman.'

Ross ignored the gibe. 'Merryck, who showed you the letter Krasner wrote to his sister?'

'The Dencourts, of course.'

And the interrogation continued, switching at random from one detail to another. Sometimes Merryck answered truthfully, sometimes he lied, but his basic story didn't waver. Nor did his questioners' disbelief. As repetition followed repetition and still they got nowhere, tempers inevitably rose.

At last Ross said, 'Okay, Merryck. I told you at the beginning we wanted straight answers and you said you understood. Seemingly you don't, so we'll have to try something else.'

He nodded at Ford who advanced on Merryck, dangling a pair of handcuffs. 'Just to make sure –' he said. 'Hold out your wrists.' He was obviously enjoying himself.

Merryck's patience was at an end. He kicked Ford in the shin. It was a brutally hard kick, expertly placed in spite of being delivered from such an awkward angle. Ford gave a howl of pain, collapsing on the floor. And Merryck launched himself at Ross.

The fight was as brief as it was pointless. Merryck had the advantage of surprise, but that was all. A warning shot that almost grazed his head stopped him cold, and he rolled free of Ross.

'Don't move, Merryck, not even an eyelash, or I'll blow your foot off,' Adamson said calmly.

Merryck lay quite still, breathing hard, waiting for what he knew was to come, but not regretting his action. He'd only precipitated the inevitable.

Fourteen

The cellar floor was rough cement. It made a hard and uncomfortable bed. Hugh Merryck, trying to ease the discomfort of his body, slowly shifted his position and at once cried out. Inadvertently he had touched the hot water pipe to which he was handcuffed, and the unlagged pipe, running from the furnace that provided the central heating for the cottage, had instantly seared his skin.

Wincing at the new pain, he let his tongue play along his thick and swollen lips. There was a taste of blood in his mouth. Gingerly he probed with the small finger of his free hand and found two loose teeth. He cursed aloud.

At least he wasn't gagged. Adamson and Ford had made it quite clear that there was no one near by to hear any shouts when, an hour ago, they had carried him down the wooden stairs and flung him into the corner by the furnace. The shot they'd fired and the noise they had already made was sufficient proof they were speaking the truth.

Ever since his brief attack had been thwarted, Merryck's wrists and ankles had all been manacled, but once Adamson had changed his cuff from left wrist to hot water pipe, he had stood back, taking care to keep well out of Merryck's reach, and released his ankles. Not that the caution was necessary. After the beating up they had given him, Merryck didn't feel like offering any further resistance.

He had lain on the ground, his body slack, only rolling slightly to one side to protect himself from the vicious parting kick that Ford had aimed at his groin. But, through slitted eyes, he had taken in as much of his surroundings as he could. By the time they left him, switching off the light at the top of the stairs, he was reasonably oriented.

A lot of good that was likely to do him, Merryck thought bitterly. He could have drawn a sketch of the cellar, the shuttered windows, the pile of neatly-chopped logs, the disused washing tubs, the newer washer and dryer, the furnace, the open stairs, the solid-looking door above. But until he could free himself, the information was quite worthless.

For a while after the two CIA men had gone, Merryck lay in the darkness, making no movement, listening hard. At first the sounds he heard told him nothing. Then he heard noise, voices that seemed to come from outside, and he recognized the slam of a car door, the revving of an engine. Someone was leaving. At least one of his enemies was departing – possibly all of them.

Ross had said they intended to leave him overnight in the cellar, in the hope that it might bring him to his senses by the following morning. Merryck grinned fiercely to himself. He had stuck to his story about the Dencourts in spite of the roughing up they'd given him and, if they thought a night on a concrete floor was going to make him change it, they'd got another think coming. In fact, though it had been bad, he'd had worse. Apart from that bloody sadist Ford, they'd been surprisingly restrained, possibly underestimating his ability to take punishment, possibly slightly unsure of their ground and unwilling to risk going too far. By tomorrow, he guessed, they'd have consulted their superiors, and they might not be so considerate. If he gave them the chance to have another go at him and they were really serious, the possibilities were endless – polygraphs, hypnosis, psychotropic drugs – the whole works.

As time passed the possibility that they'd have their chance grew stronger. The handcuff was clearly unbreakable. The hot water pipe was firmly fixed and resisted all his efforts to shift it. He'd been thoroughly searched – even his nail file had been removed – and there was no sort of weapon or tool within reach.

Temporarily Merryck desisted. He was breathing hard

and sweat trickled down his face. He was exhausting himself and achieving nothing. He was no nearer freeing himself than when he'd started struggling with the damned pipe. All he'd managed to do was burn his hand rather badly.

Nevertheless, he was about to recommence his efforts when, as if to mock him, he heard the opening bars of what he thought was a Brahms piano sonata. Whoever had driven away from the cottage, it was not Ken Ford. Ford, obviously left on guard, was indulging in his favourite pastime.

Merryck gritted his teeth. The music irked him. He pictured Ford sitting at the old upright – it was slightly out of tune – imagining himself at Carnegie Hall. Angrily, knowing it was useless, he again began to tug and jerk at the cuff on his wrist until eventually, frustrated and weary, he admitted temporary defeat.

He was wondering whether he could devise some ruse to lure Ford down to the cellar and persuade him to come close enough to be vulnerable to another attack, when there was a discordant jangle of notes from upstairs, and the music ceased abruptly. Merryck heaved a sigh of relief. The next instant he was tense. The silence was shattered by a sudden staccato succession of shots.

He strained to listen, astounded at this turn of events, asking himself if he could conceivably have mistaken the noise of gunfire, but convinced that he hadn't. He could hear nothing now but the sound of his own breathing and the thump of his heart. Minutes later there was a faint squeak as the door at the top of the cellar stairs was quietly opened. A powerful flashlight flicked round the cellar, pausing for a moment on him. He lay motionless as an electric light switch clicked and brightness flooded his prison, feigning unconsciousness until he could judge what might happen next.

The stairs creaked, and through half-closed eyes Merryck watched two pairs of legs descending rapidly. They came and stood over him. A foot kicked him gently. Hands reached down and turned him over on to his back. Merryck groaned aloud. And, above him, someone swore fluently, in German.

Merryck was not unduly surprised. He groaned again, made his eyelids flutter and slowly opened them. He found himself looking up into the face of the GDR man he'd dubbed Duffel Coat. The second man, Blue Raincoat, was hurrying back up the stairs.

'It's all right, Mr Merryck. Lie still. You'll be free very soon,' Duffel Coat said in English.

Merryck obeyed. It was pointless to speculate on the train of events that had brought the couple to the cottage. Perhaps the CIA team had been followed from New York; perhaps the GDR men had been in the dark grey car behind Martha and himself. What was more puzzling was their behaviour. On some occasions they operated in a casual, amateurish fashion, and on others they showed astonishing resource and efficiency. Merryck could scarcely complain at their presence now, but that didn't mean he really liked it. He warned himself to be very wary of them.

'Here we are. Dietrich has brought the key to the handcuffs.'

'And some brandy, Karl. Mr Merryck is awake? Good. The sooner we are away from here the better.'

'*Jawohl.* Before Mr Merryck's CIA friends return.'

As they carried on this curiously stilted conversation, the man whose name seemed to be Dietrich released the cuff from the hot water pipe, and immediately clasped it around Merryck's other wrist. Merryck stifled a cry as the hot metal touched his flesh, and Dietrich half-mumbled an apology. Then together the Germans helped Merryck to sit up and sip the brandy. But they were very careful. They took no risks and, even though he was pretending to be considerably weaker than he felt, Merryck estimated his chances of getting the better of them as nil.

'Can you walk, Mr Merryck?'

'Sure. Or at least I can try.'

Accepting their assistance, Merryck got slowly to his feet. As far as he could see, there was no purpose in trying to delay the Germans, but he must find out what had happened to

Ken Ford. There had been shooting. If Ford had been badly hurt . . .

When they reached the top of the cellar stairs, he said, 'I can't go like this. I've a coat and a big bag and there are all the things from my pockets. I can't go without them. And my face – and hands. I must clean up.'

Karl inspected him. 'Your injuries are not serious, Mr Merryck. Cleaning up must wait. There's no time for that. But your things – yes. You will need those. Where are they?'

'In the living-room, I expect.'

'Right. Come along then. We will find them. But we must be quick.'

The three of them went through the archway into the living-room. The East Germans, who knew what to expect, were unmoved, but Merryck hesitated automatically. Ken Ford was lying, face upwards, beside the overturned piano-stool. His face was a mess of blood and flesh. The top of his head had been shot away, and some of his brain was spattered on the piano keys. Merryck felt his gorge rise. He turned angrily on his rescuers.

'Why in hell did you have to kill him?'

'Steady, Mr Merryck. Steady. It was self-defence. Either him or us.'

Knowing that this was possibly the truth didn't improve Merryck's temper. 'And I suppose that's why you killed the old man in Bonn – Gerhardt, Klaus Gerhardt. In self-defence?'

'*Nein*. Gerhardt got a good price for Martha Schmidt's letter, but he came back for more. He'd become a liability.'

While duffel-coated Karl was speaking, Dietrich had collected Merryck's possessions. Wallet, passport, keys, loose change, watch, even his special pocket knife, Dietrich stuffed them all into various pockets of Merryck's jacket. The ski-cap he jammed on Merryck's head. The car-coat he hung round Merryck's shoulders.

Standing there, being dressed like a child, Merryck longed to bring his knee up into the man's groin. He hadn't liked

Ken Ford, who was clearly a highly temperamental guy, far less predictable than either Ross or Adamson, but he hadn't wished him dead. And his death was a further, appalling complication.

'There you are. Now we're ready. Let us go, Mr Merryck. I will bring your bag.'

Ready for what? Go where? Merryck wished he had some answers. But his first objective – to put a lot of distance between himself and Ford's body – he clearly shared with the East Germans, and to achieve this he was prepared to co-operate with them. Then he must do his best to get rid of the GDR men. After that, he wasn't sure. And what Messrs Karl and Dietrich might have in mind for him was anyone's guess.

Outside the cottage, Merryck was surprised to find that dusk was only just falling. In the shuttered darkness of the cellar, without any means of knowing the time, he had assumed it was much later and already dark. He followed in the footsteps of one German, the other behind him occasionally giving him a helping hand as he purposely stumbled.

In fact, when they had left the path to the front door, Merryck, his hands still manacled, found it increasingly difficult to keep his balance. They skirted a shrubbery, went around to the back of the house and set off across a field to a belt of trees bordering the ice-covered lake he had noticed when he first arrived. They were following what seemed to be a well-worn track, but at times the snow was over the tops of their shoes, and walking was difficult and unpleasant. Fortunately, the actual distance was short.

Hidden among the trees just off a narrow road was the dark grey car that Merryck had last seen keeping its distance behind Martha. Merryck was hustled into the back, his hold-all at his feet. Karl sat beside him, half-turned to face him, his right hand bulging ominously in the pocket of his duffel coat. Dietrich drove.

'Where are you taking me?' Merryck asked finally.

'To Toronto – downtown Toronto. Do you know the city, Mr Merryck?'

'No.'

'Then I think we will drop you at the corner of Bloor Street and Avenue Road. Bloor is the – what shall I say? – the Kurfürstendamm, perhaps, the rue de la Paix, the Bond Street of Toronto. It runs east and west, Avenue Road north and south. There's an excellent hotel at the intersection, and everything else you're likely to want.'

Merryck stared at him. 'You mean you're going to stop in some public place with people around, open the car door, hand me my bag and drive off?'

'That's right, Mr Merryck. We will remove your hand-cuffs first, of course.'

'But why? You're crazy! You must be kidding.'

'No, Mr Merryck. Perhaps we're not always as efficient as we would like to be – we lost you for a whole weekend in New York, for instance. Our only excuse is that it's hard to operate in a foreign country, where adequate back-up isn't always available at short notice. But we're not crazy. We've no real quarrel with you, Mr Merryck, and we're glad of the opportunity to release you from the hands of your – allies, shall I say? Neither are we playing games, Mr Merryck. As I said, we've no wish to hurt you, but if you try to do anything stupid while you're in this automobile I shall be forced to put a bullet in your kneecap. Very painful, I'm told, and it never really heals.'

Merryck laughed. 'You can put that gun away if you're taking me to Toronto. Why should I stop you giving me a lift?' Then he added mildly, 'But what makes you think I won't go to the police as soon as you drop me – if you do.'

Karl said, 'Oh, we will, I assure you, Mr Merryck. And use your brains. You may be in Canada now, but that won't help you much. Can you think of any credible story you can tell the Toronto Metropolitan Police, the Ontario Provincial Police, and eventually the Royal Canadian Mounted Police? Don't forget there's a body to account for.' He laughed in his

143

turn. 'No, Mr Merryck, my advice to you is to keep away from all the police forces unless you want to end up in custody.'

Merryck was silent. It was the truth, and it was bitter. Quite apart from the security of his mission, there was no way he could approach the authorities. Without Ross's support, they wouldn't believe him and, with Ford dead, Ross would be in no mood to help him. If he weren't accused of murder he'd certainly be held as a possible accessory. At best he'd spend time in a Toronto gaol, and when he got out – if he got out – Otto Krasner would have gone on an extended holiday. Not even his daughter would know where. The house would be shut up . . .

Merryck's thoughts rioted. The house in York Mills – that was his one trump card, his one current asset. Martha had let slip the fact that the family home was there, and the full address had been on her mother's letters. It was an odds-on bet that Krasner was there at this very moment, with Martha. And Ross? Perhaps. Perhaps not. He'd have to risk Ross. The sooner he got to Krasner the better, before anything was known of Ford's death, before the alarm bells in the CIA started ringing.

But what of the GDR men, the unfunny team of Karl and Dietrich, Duffel Coat and Blue Raincoat, who killed without a qualm? In spite of what they said, they weren't going to drop him on some well-populated Toronto street corner and wave him a cheerful goodbye. What did they expect him to do? Continue to look for Krasner, presumably. They had no reason to believe he knew where Krasner was, but they might suspect he had a better idea than they did. In that case, why hadn't they in their turn had a go at interrogating him? Why hadn't they also tried some roughing up? Perhaps they preferred more devious methods . . .

Merryck gave up. He could only await events. When the crunch came, if it did, he'd have to balance the need for speed in reaching Krasner against the need to make sure he wasn't blowing Krasner's cover to the GDR.

In spite of the powerful heater in the car, Merryck was shivering. His shoes and socks were soaked, and his feet were like blocks of ice. Apart from the brandy he'd been given in the cellar, it was a long time since he'd had anything to eat or drink – and he'd been beaten up in the interval. By now his mouth had ceased to ache, but his burnt hand and wrist throbbed continuously. He thought longingly of a hot bath and an enormous pot of coffee, and stared disconsolately out of the window.

There was little to be seen, though it had been obvious for some time that they were taking a different route south, for the highway wasn't divided and it passed through a succession of villages and small towns. A scattering of snow had fallen as darkness came, and Dietrich was driving carefully, though fast. Once or twice he slowed as they approached a Fina or Texaco sign, but for some reason decided not to stop. Eventually, however, on the outskirts of a place that seemed to be called Aurora, he drew up in the forecourt of a service station, though well beyond the brightly-lighted pump area.

'Be quick,' his companion ordered. 'And you, Mr Merryck, remember what I said. Don't do anything to draw attention to yourself. Dietrich won't be long. He's only gone to use the toilet.'

Merryck glanced over his shoulder as another car pulled up behind them, and the attendant came out to the pumps. For an instant he considered the possibility of an escape attempt, but as instantly rejected it. What was the point?

'I could do with a pee myself,' he said lightly.

Karl grunted. 'It's not too far now, Mr Merryck. But there'll be more light as we enter the city, and we will have to slow or stop more often in traffic. So keep your handcuffs under your coat. We don't want any accidents, do we?'

Merryck bit off the answer he was about to make as Dietrich returned. He had nothing to gain by provoking the East Germans. Better to play docile. Hunching his shoulders, he pretended to doze, but watched as snowy country became grey suburb, and suburbia gave way to city streets.

And, after a while, Karl said, 'We are almost there, Mr Merryck. We are coming down Avenue Road towards the city centre. Bloor Street is about six blocks ahead. Listen carefully. This is what we will do. As Dietrich draws in to the kerb I will release your handcuffs. Immediately you will open your door and slip out. I will hand you your bag. Three quick movements, remember. Don't do anything stupid. My aim might not be so good from a moving vehicle and you could easily end up dead. I doubt if you're being paid enough to make that risk worth taking.' He gave a sardonic grin. 'Ready now?'

'I'm ready.'

Seconds later Merryck was standing on the pavement, his teeth beginning to chatter, as the grey car accelerated across the intersection and disappeared into the distance. Scarcely able to credit what had happened Merryck looked swiftly about him. According to the street signs he was, as the Germans had promised, on the corner of Bloor Street West and Avenue Road. All around were bright lights, tall buildings, shops closed or about to close for the night, streams of moving traffic on the two wide roads, hurrying pedestrians. The snow had ceased but everything was covered with a thin sprinkling of white. To Merryck it was a magical scene, despite the cold.

A taxi was parked at the kerb some twenty-five yards up the road and, as he looked in its direction, it began to move. He waved. For a moment he thought the driver was going to ignore him, but then with a squeal of brakes the cab drew up.

The driver wound down his window. 'Where to?' he said abruptly. 'I'm going off duty.'

Merryck hesitated, but surely a planted cab would be less reluctant. 'York Mills,' he said carefully. 'Do you know it?'

'Sure.' The driver eyed Merryck dubiously. 'But it's a fair

ways from here and I don't know the district too well.'

'Look, it's terribly important I get there. I'll double your fare.'

'Okay then.' He leaned over the back of his seat and opened the cab door.

'Thanks.'

Merryck pulled up the coat that was slipping from his shoulders, threw his hold-all into the cab and climbed in after it. He slammed the door, wincing. Getting out of the East Germans' car he'd been too occupied to think about his hand and his wrist, which by now had turned an unpleasant purplish-red colour, and were swollen and blistered. He looked at them with distaste, and wondered again about the rest of his appearance. He'd had no chance to see his face in a mirror, but he could guess it was as unprepossessing as his hands. At the thought, Merryck's remaining suspicions about the cab were lulled; his driver's initial reluctance to accept him as a fare hadn't been some kind of double-bluff, but had a reasonable explanation. He must look a fairly disreputable wreck.

But that didn't mean he trusted the GDR men. Though they'd driven off exactly as they said they would, Merryck still expected to see them again though not necessarily in the same grey car. He could think of no reason why they should rescue him from the CIA, then let him go completely free. Shrugging off his coat and pushing back his ski-cap, Merryck savoured the warmth of the cab, and turned to watch the traffic behind.

His cab had turned right, right and right again before turning left to retrace the route north up Avenue Road. He was a good driver, and his manœuvre had been quick and skilful – in itself enough to shake any but the most accomplished tail. Certainly there were no obvious signs of any following vehicle.

'York Mills,' said the cabbie suddenly. 'Address?' he added.

Merryck named the street. 'But drive around a few blocks

147

when you get there,' he said. 'I want to see what the neighbourhood's like.'

'Okay,' said the driver. 'They're your dollars.' Then a few minutes later he went on, 'I'll have to stop and look at the map. I told you I don't know this area too well.'

Merryck raised no objection. Parked under a light while the driver, whistling through his teeth, studied a street guide, he had an excellent opportunity to make sure that no one was taking any sort of interest in them.

'Got it!' the driver said at last.

'Fine. Let's go then.'

'What's the number?'

'Just drop me anywhere on the road.'

'Okay. Okay. But you might have a long walk.'

By this time, they had come to a district of curving, tree-lined streets with large and imposing houses of varied architectural styles, each set well back in good-sized gardens – grounds, almost. The recent new snow formed a soft white sheet over the ground and the trees and the shrubberies. It had not yet been cleared from the road, and tyre marks showed the passage of occasional traffic.

The cab came to a halt at a road junction. 'This do?' the driver asked. 'The street you want goes back three blocks the way we've come, and four blocks straight ahead – and they're big blocks, especially carrying that bag.' He nodded at Merryck's hold-all.

Merryck paid no attention to the implied hint. 'This is fine,' he said. Trying to disregard the pain of his burnt hand, he extracted a twenty-dollar bill from his wallet. 'Twenty dollars US? Is that all right? I've only got American.'

'Great,' said the driver. 'I'm not patriotic.' It was the first really unnecessary comment he'd made since they left Bloor and Avenue Road.

Merryck climbed painfully from the taxi and took his bag. 'Thanks,' he said.

'You're welcome.'

The taxi-driver wasted no time. He moved off at once,

turning left at the intersection. Merryck waited until he could no longer hear the noise of the engine, and then surveyed his surroundings more closely. In spite of its almost rural atmosphere the street was well lit, and the houses – which in England would almost certainly have had names – displayed their numbers, usually with wrought-iron signs. A short reconnaissance showed Merryck that he'd probably been dropped within a couple of hundred yards of the Krasner's home, and he set out towards it.

The house, when he found it, was modern, as Martha had said, and long and low. Merryck paused beside a bare tree on the other side of the road and inspected it carefully. It was apparently occupied; at least four of the many ground-floor windows showed light behind their drawn curtains. The garage was open, with two cars in it and a vacant space for another. One of the cars was the Chevrolet Martha had rented at Toronto airport. The second was presumably Krasner's. Did the absence of any other vehicles indicate that they were alone? Merryck had no way of knowing.

There was very little cover around the house and between it and its neighbours, neither of which showed any lights at all, and no signs of surveillance in the area. Merryck walked slowly up the drive, his silent feet making the first footprints in the carpet of snow. He moved round the house under the windows, and was lucky. The curtains screening one of the lighted windows had been carelessly drawn.

Cautiously he raised his head above the sill. Martha and her father were sitting opposite each other before a fire, drinking what must surely be their after-dinner coffee. Why they were so apparently unprotected and vulnerable, Merryck couldn't fathom. Possibly over the years the authorities – the CIA and the Canadians – had been careful to avoid drawing attention to Krasner, and saw no reason to change this policy in the light of recent events. After all, as far as they were concerned, Krasner's Toronto address was still a closely-guarded secret.

Merryck considered his options as he shivered in the cold night air. There was nothing for it but direct action. He moved quietly back along the front of the house to the main door, and simply rang the bell.

Fifteen

'Hugh!'

'Hello, Martha.' His voice was controlled and casual.

She stared at him, incredulous, disconcerted, eyes wide, lips parted. His face was swollen and smeared with blood, his thick car-coat slipped from one shoulder. He clutched his canvas hold-all in his right hand. In spite of the ridiculous ski-cap perched on the back of his head, his appearance was baleful, even menacing. Martha drew in a deep breath, and for a moment Merryck thought she was about to slam the door on him. Immediately he pushed past her into the hall.

'It's okay, Martha.' Now he spoke savagely. 'I'm not a ghost. I'm still very much alive – in spite of the treatment your CIA chums gave me.'

Martha swallowed hard. 'Hugh,' she said hoarsely. 'Hugh, I'm sorry. I didn't know ... Believe me, please. I didn't know ... Steve said ...'

She stopped, faltering, as Merryck dropped his bag on the hall carpet, and shrugged his coat on top of it. He held out his hands and wrists so that she could see the blistered burn marks. But before she could respond someone called to her. 'Martha, sweetie, who is it? Is something wrong?' It was a light baritone voice, a little frail and anxious, with no trace of European accent.

'That's Dad,' Martha said helplessly.

'Good!' Merryck was in no mood to be sympathetic. 'I'm glad to be meeting him at last. You two are alone here?'

Martha hesitated. 'Yes,' she said at length. 'Quite alone. Hugh, you won't –'

'Martha! What is it?'

'Coming, Dad.' Martha gave Merryck an appealing glance. 'You're alone, too?'

'I'm alone, Martha. I'm unarmed. And, for the umpteenth time, I don't intend your father any harm.' He pulled off his ski-cap and dropped it on to his coat. 'I'm also bloody tired after all the hoops you've had me jumping through. I just don't want any more nonsense from you or the Agency or –'

As he spoke Merryck brushed passed her, turned left through a wide arch and went down two steps into the room from which the voice had come. It was a long room, both elegant and comfortable, with an open hearth and a blazing log fire. To one side of the fire an elderly man sat in a deep armchair.

Otto Krasner at last! Older, thinner, greyer than his photograph in Martha's New York apartment, but nevertheless the man he'd been seeking. The distant stranger, Merryck thought with a sense of anti-climax, surprised at his lack of excitement.

Behind him, Martha said, 'Dad, this is Hugh Merryck. I don't know how he –'

'Ah yes. How are you, Mr Merryck? Forgive me for not standing up to greet you, but I avoid unnecessary exertion these days.' Krasner was calm and apparently unperturbed. It could have been an ordinary social occasion. 'Do sit down,' he continued. 'I hope you don't find the room too hot but, pointless as it is with central heating, I do enjoy a good fire in the evening at this time of year.' His voice might show no trace of his European origins, but his phraseology was English, rather than North American.

'Thank you.' Merryck, matching courtesy with courtesy, but conscious of his disreputable appearance and the trail of damp footprints he'd left on the light carpet, sat in an armchair opposite Krasner. 'I apologize for arriving uninvited like this, Mr Krasner, but I need to talk to you very badly.'

'So I've been informed, Mr Merryck. Incidentally, please

don't use that name. It's ages since I answered to it. I've been Carlton for twenty –'

'Dad, for God's sake!' Martha, who had been standing just inside the room, could bear this slow-moving exchange no longer. 'Dad! We should call Steve.'

'No.' Merryck and Krasner spoke in unison. Then Krasner added, 'It's too late, sweetie. If you call Steve Mr Merryck will walk out, and my next visitors could prove far less acceptable, perhaps the Press, perhaps even my former compatriots.'

'No, not them,' Merryck said quickly.

Krasner raised his head. 'I'm glad to hear that,' he said quietly. Then, 'Anyway, Martha, let's see what Mr Merryck wants.'

'We know, Dad. Or at least we know what he'll tell us – about this Englishman Francis Dencourt – Sir Francis Dencourt. But Steve says it's all lies.' Martha sounded a little hesitant.

'Steve could be wrong. Forget Steve for the moment. Mr. Merryck is here and I'm quite prepared to discuss Francis Dencourt with him, if that's what he wants. In fact, I don't have any option, unless we're prepared to arrange for Mr Merryck to be silenced for good – and that might not be too easy. Let's see if we can't strike a bargain with him instead.'

Merryck was watching Krasner with interest. He found the contradiction between the bland mask of a face and the incisive urbane mind somewhat bewildering. He supposed that Krasner's family and friends were accustomed to it. Or was Krasner, finding himself in a tight corner, revealing more of his true self than usual?

Krasner glanced from Martha to Merryck, and continued. 'But first, let's be practical. Mr Merryck is not, I think, in very good shape. His face looks dreadful, his feet are obviously soaking – and his hands?'

'Burnt,' Merryck said briefly.

'Badly? Do they need medical attention?'

'Not now. Not immediately.'

Krasner nodded. 'As you say, Mr Merryck. So – are you hungry? Thirsty? I'm afraid we've eaten, but –'

'Both.'

'I see. Well, Martha will pour us each a large whisky. I'm sure you can manage to hold a glass. Then –'

Some twenty minutes later Merryck was considerably more comfortable. Martha had led the way to the cloakroom, and produced towels and a pair of her father's slippers. A piece of plaster hid his cut lip, and his hand and wrist had been treated. As Martha knelt before him to bandage them, Merryck had been unable to resist the temptation to lean forward and kiss the top of her head. She had looked up at him without speaking, before hastening away to cook him an omelette. Merryck wondered if, out of his sight, she would make her phone call, but a moment's reflection persuaded him that trust was the only feasible policy. Now, back in his chair opposite Krasner, he was planning the form of his questions.

Krasner said, 'That's much better, Mr Merryck. You look almost human again, if I may say so.' Then he added unexpectedly, 'This is all my fault, you know. You'd never have found me if I hadn't broken the Agency's instructions.'

'You mean they didn't know you were writing to your sister?' Merryck was incredulous. 'Surely –'

'Oh yes, they knew all right. I'd been pestering them for a long time. I was very fond of my sister, and I hated the idea of her thinking me dead for all those years.' Krasner fell silent, lost in memories.

'So,' Merryck prompted at length.

'So, as soon as her husband died, they gave me permission to write – for some reason they never trusted my brother-in-law. But they laid down stringent rules, and insisted on seeing the letters. I had to make it quite clear to Martha how she must treat the one-sided correspondence. I told her that if she didn't do as I said the letters would stop immediately, and I'd be in danger. I always suspected that the Agency found ways of reinforcing my warnings.'

Merryck said, 'But it was just chance your last letter was stolen. No one was to blame – except the man who stole it, and he's dead.'

Krasner didn't seem interested in the death of Klaus Gerhardt. Continuing with his own train of thought, he went on, 'My mistake was to give Lotte's name and address to my sister. It was the only letter I posted myself, the only one Steve Ross didn't see. Steve assured me Martha was all right, but I wasn't convinced. After all, she was getting on in years, and I wanted her to have a way of contacting me if she was ever in need.' Suddenly Krasner's voice became edged with irritation. 'Instead the fool woman had to go and send our mother's brooch to Lotte as a present for Martha. Otherwise you'd never have traced me. Never. So, after all these years I've brought you here myself.'

Merryck said nothing. He felt a certain sympathy for Krasner. Nevertheless, he wished the old man would talk of his escape from East Germany and the involvement of the then British Ambassador, rather than about his sister and himself. He guessed, however, that it would be a mistake to try to hurry him. It looked as if Krasner was prepared to co-operate, but on his own terms, as and when he chose.

Merryck contained his impatience, grateful when Martha brought him supper on a tray. Despite his bruised and swollen face, he ate ravenously and drank three large cups of coffee. Conversation was minimal. Mostly Krasner stared into the fire, brooding, and Martha turned the pages of a *Maclean*'s magazine. Merryck concentrated on his food.

'Thank you very much,' he said as he finished. 'That was just what I needed. It was a wonderful meal.' He leaned back in his comfortable chair.

Martha smiled, but as she took the tray the front doorbell rang. Merryck's immediate reaction was that Martha had in fact phoned Ross.

He was about to rise to his feet, when Krasner said, 'Ah, that will be Mrs Dobson. My housekeeper,' he explained for Merryck's benefit. 'She said she'd be back tonight if she didn't telephone. She's been visiting a sick daughter in Oshawa.'

'Doesn't she have her own key?' Merryck asked, still slightly doubtful.

'Of course. But she knows we keep the chain on the door at night,' Krasner replied.

He appeared to be listening. There had been some sounds in the hall, but no women's voices raised in greeting. Suddenly Merryck saw him stiffen, his knuckles white as he gripped the arms of his chair, the colour draining from his face. Merryck turned his head and swore under his breath. The only excuses for his incompetence were fatigue, and the relaxation induced by his meal. At the first ring of the bell he should have acted – concealed himself, at least moved to the inner side of the entrance archway. Now he was vulnerable, and for the moment at a frustrating tactical disadvantage.

Martha was standing at the top of the two steps leading down from the hall. The man whom Merryck knew as Karl was behind her, an arm locked around her throat, holding her close against him. With his free hand he pressed a pistol into her temple. A second man – who earlier had driven Merryck to York Mills in his cab – stood to one side, covering Krasner and Merryck with a revolver. God! thought Merryck. What a set-up! Dietrich must have fixed it by phone from that petrol station.

Then Krasner made an inarticulate noise in his throat, and all eyes automatically turned towards him; even the GDR men were momentarily distracted. Merryck, seizing his opportunity, sprang to his feet, but Karl swung round on him.

'Stop – exactly where you are, Mr Merryck. And don't try any heroics if you value Miss Krasner's life.'

'My name's not Krasner. I'm Martha Carlton, and you're hurting me.'

Merryck felt a flash of admiration for Martha's courage, useless though he knew her protestations would be. And it was his fault, Merryck acknowledged bitterly – it was due to him that the GDR were here at all. He'd blown Krasner's cover.

Furious at the way he'd allowed himself to be duped, Merryck was tempted to fling himself at Karl, but there was no point in endangering Martha for the sake of an empty gesture. Better to wait and hope for a chance later. He stayed on his feet, but deliberately let his shoulders slouch, holding his bandaged hand and wrist before him pathetically. The GDR men would kill when they had to – they'd already proved that at the cottage – but at least they hadn't burst in firing indiscriminately; they weren't even equipped with the right sort of automatic weapons for such an operation. Clearly, they didn't intend to dispose of Krasner immediately. They wanted something first. And that meant delay. And any delay could change the odds so that they weren't so hopelessly unbalanced.

But not too long, Merryck added to himself – I can't wait too long. When they've got what they want, or they're sure they can't get it, Krasner and Martha and I will all be killed, Krasner because of his past, and Martha and I because we're expendable.

'What do you want?' Krasner had recovered his wits in the few seconds it had taken Merryck to reach this conclusion, though his voice was raw. 'Whatever it is you can have it – and that includes my life, or such of it as remains – but first release my daughter.'

'Suppose we start with this book you're writing, Herr Krasner – your memoirs,' said Karl. 'Let us see what you have to say about our Fatherland, for instance.'

'When you've released my daughter.' Krasner spoke firmly.

'Krasner, we're not here to bargain. The memoirs – now! We've no time to waste.' Karl tightened his grip on Martha, and jammed the pistol hard against her head so that she cried out with pain. 'Otherwise I'll kill her at once.'

'Stay there! He means it! He'll shoot!'

As Krasner made to rise from his chair Merryck inter-

vened hurriedly, terrified that Martha's father would precipitate some crisis that could only end in immediate disaster. He himself took advantage of the momentary confusion
caused by his sudden shout to edge around a small table on
which lay a heavy glass paperweight. He was also several
steps nearer to the East Germans who had advanced into the
room. Merryck's position had improved marginally.

'The memoirs!' Karl demanded again.

'In my bedroom, along the corridor,' Krasner told him
reluctantly, subsiding back into his chair. 'There's an old
desk.'

'The girl knows where they are?'

'Yes. I'll show you.' Martha spoke for herself. To
Merryck's relief she sounded quite calm. 'But please don't
hold me so tightly.'

'Very well. But try any tricks and you're dead.' Karl
pushed her ahead of him up the two steps and into the hall,
saying over his shoulder, 'Watch them, Heinrich. Don't trust
them.'

'Don't worry.'

The erstwhile taxi-driver's eyes flicked from Krasner to
Merryck, and back again to Krasner. To him, Otto Krasner
was the important prisoner, a man who had betrayed his
country, the reason why he and Karl were engaged on this
operation. Merryck was almost a bystander, merely a non-
threatening figure who'd been tricked into leading them to
Krasner. He didn't ignore Merryck, but he concentrated the
greater part of his attention on Krasner. It was his mistake.

In apparent despondency Merryck watched Karl and
Martha disappear along the hall. This, he knew, could be his
chance, possibly the only one he'd get. The odds had tipped
fractionally in his favour. If he failed, he'd never know; he'd
be dead within seconds. Soon to be followed, no doubt, by
Krasner and Martha.

As these thoughts fled through his mind Merryck, his
battered face continuing to express utter dejection, moved
his right arm behind him. His fingers closed firmly round the

paperweight, and with his eye he measured the distance to the gun held steady in Heinrich's hand. If he missed . . .

Without warning Krasner broke into a paroxysm of coughing. Either he'd seen Merryck grope for the paperweight and realized what was intended or it was coincidence. Whatever the reason, he drew the GDR man's attention from Merryck. And Merryck brought his arm round and hurled the paperweight at the East German's gun hand with all the force he could muster.

His aim was perfect. The paperweight caught the German on the wrist, and the gun spun away. Almost before he could cry out Merryck was on him, not waiting to get close but kicking high. Heinrich's windpipe was shattered. He died instantly.

The whole incident had taken only seconds and had been surprisingly silent. Hurriedly Merryck picked up the gun and dragged the body to a part of the room that wouldn't immediately be within Karl's field of vision as he entered.

'Keep your eyes fixed on him, as if he'd still got a gun,' he whispered to Krasner.

Krasner nodded his understanding. 'Martha?' he mouthed desperately.

Merryck managed to produce what he hoped was an encouraging smile. They were far from out of the woods, and Martha was now in the most danger. He went and stood inside the archway, his back against the wall.

In less than a minute he heard Karl returning. Clearly unaware of what had happened in his absence, the East German moved confidently, propelling Martha in front of him and turning into the living-room without hesitation. Martha was carrying a bulging file – presumably her father's memoirs – and the East German was slightly off balance on the second of the two steps when he felt the chill of his compatriot's gun muzzle at his neck.

'Hold it!' Merryck snapped out the words like a sergeant-major.

Karl froze, his glance taking in the changed situation,

Krasner still in his chair, but Heinrich's body on the carpet. He said calmly, 'I shan't hesitate to kill the girl, you know.'

'And I wouldn't hesitate to shoot you either.'

There was a pause, then the GDR man shrugged. 'So, what do you suggest, Mr Merryck? We have an impasse – a stand-off, do you call it? What can we do to resolve it?'

It was an almost classical problem, and Merryck had foreseen it. He was also conscious that Dietrich, the third East German, could well be somewhere outside the house. Any undue delay might bring him on to the scene.

He said, 'I'll make a bargain with you. Release Miss Carlton and throw down your gun. I'll throw down mine at the same time. Then you can take your cab-driver chum and clear out.'

Even as he spoke Merryck knew his ploy was a waste of time. Karl was shaking with seeming laughter. 'You mean we should trust each other, Mr Merryck?' he said incredulously. He made the suggestion sound preposterous.

'What else?' Merryck was grim.

The answer was supplied by Otto Krasner. With a strangled cry he pitched out of his chair on to the hearth. Martha screamed. She threw the file she was carrying away from her into the middle of the room, stamped backwards with all her strength on to Karl's shin and, regardless of her safety, wrenched herself free. Her only thought was to get to her father.

The consequences were far-reaching. Karl, caught unawares by Martha's sudden and violent attack, was spun around, the automatic knocked out of his hand. Merryck with a well-aimed kick sent it spinning to a far corner of the room.

'Hugh! Help! Help me! Quick!' Martha's cry was urgent, demanding.

Merryck hesitated, but only for a split second. Krasner had fallen into the hearth, and his fall had dislodged the burning logs. One was beside his head, a second by his arm. Others were on the carpet, sending fiery sparks up to the mantel. There was a smell of singeing – of cloth? Of hair? Of flesh? Still clutching his gun, Merryck raced across the room to drag Krasner clear.

For his part Karl didn't hesitate at all. Instantly appreciating the changed circumstances, he ran to his dead compatriot. Luckily Heinrich was slightly-built, and Karl was able to sling the body over one shoulder. Then, grabbing the file as he passed, he dashed for the front door. No one tried to stop him.

By now the emergency was over. Krasner was unharmed, apart from a singed coat sleeve. The logs had been kicked back into the fire and the sparks on the carpet extinguished. Martha had found her father's heart pills, and was fetching water. Together they helped Krasner to take the drugs, then got him back into his chair. His face, colourless before, was now grey, and he seemed to be improving.

'I'll call the doctor,' said Martha.

'No, don't. There's nothing he can do. It was just a sharp pain – one of my attacks.' Otto Krasner's grimace was a good attempt at a smile. 'I'm all right now.'

'You must go to bed, Dad.'

'Stop fussing, girl. I'll – I'll go in a moment. Shut the front door. That bastard didn't have the manners to shut it himself and it's – it's draughty.'

Martha looked at her father anxiously, then went to shut the door. Merryck collected Karl's gun, picking it up carefully by the barrel, and followed her into the hall. He found a dirty shirt in his hold-all and wrapped the gun in it. While Martha automatically hung up his car coat in the hall closet, he buried the packet at the bottom of his bag.

When they returned to the living-room, Merryck said, 'I brought your enemies here, sir. I'm truly sorry. Please believe me when I say I did it unwittingly.'

'I believe you. You killed one of them.' Krasner gave Merryck a long, speculative look. 'Who are you really? British SIS?'

'No. I told you –'

Impatiently Krasner waved away the expected repetition, as the telephone rang. He said to Martha, 'If that's Steve, tell him he's too late. He's missed the show.'

In fact it was Mrs Dobson apologizing for the lateness of her call. There had been a storm in that part of Ontario and power and phone lines had been down. 'Is everything all right?' she asked.

'Fine,' said Martha, biting her bottom lip to stop her voice shaking. 'Everything's just fine, Mrs Dobson. I'm here for the weekend, so come back whenever you like. How is your daughter?'

Martha listened, murmuring her thanks to Merryck when he brought her a glass of brandy. He said to Krasner, 'I'm afraid they got your memoirs.'

'That doesn't matter,' said Krasner. 'I've another copy.' Then to Martha, who had put down the phone, 'You took that man to the bedroom –'

'Yes, just as you said. I gave him the top copy you were working on. The carbon's in the study. He didn't ask about copies, though I can't think why not.'

'Maybe they just want to see what's been written,' suggested Merryck. 'Copies may not matter to them. If they do matter –' He paused, uncertain how to continue.

'I know, I know,' said Krasner. 'If they want the copy they'll be back to try and find it. Anyway, they'll be after me. This will mean big changes, Martha, now I've been found.' He sank back in his chair.

'Bed?' said Merryck.

'Yes.' Otto Krasner struggled to his feet, and Merryck gave him an arm. 'Thanks. We'll talk tomorrow. I've had enough for today. Though I can tell you right now that in my view your Ambassador Dencourt should have been shot for what he did. Not to me – I was lucky – but to poor Johann Meissener –'

'Dad.' Martha interrupted. 'Bed! I'm going to phone Steve. We should tell him what's happened.'

'Not tonight.' Krasner shook his head. 'If you do he'll be

around asking questions and I'll get no sleep for hours.'

'But, Dad –'

'No, Martha. Wait till morning. Nothing more's going to happen tonight.' Suddenly he gave a genuine grin. 'Anyway, why should we want Steve when we've got Hugh Merryck here?'

Sixteen

Merryck stirred restlessly. Martha, asleep beside him, had turned on her back and her arm had moved on his bare chest. Last night, after they had seen her father safely to bed in his room downstairs on the ground floor, she had taken Merryck by the hand and led him without comment to her own room. She had fetched his bag from the hall, and helped him to undress. Their love-making had of necessity been gentle and of volition tender. Then, overriding his intention to stay awake and on guard, she had persuaded him to take a couple of pain-killers. As a result he had slept heavily, and now was in that no-man's-land between sleep and waking, warm, comfortable. He had no desire to take any action, but . . .

Suddenly he was fully awake. He sat up and switched on the bedside light. The room was hazy, and he could smell smoke in his nostrils. Shouting to Martha, Merryck leapt from the bed and ran naked to the door. He opened it cautiously. The corridor was full of acrid greyness, and he could hear the distant crackle of flame. The fire, wherever its centre, was well alight.

His eyes already watering, Merryck dashed into the adjoining bathroom and seized a towel. Hastily he dampened it under the shower, ran back through the bedroom and stuffed it under the door. It should keep out some of the smoke and give them a little time. He saw with relief that Martha was awake. She had thrown aside the sheets and was getting out of bed.

'What is it, Hugh? What is it?'

'Fire!' He wrenched open a clothes closet and threw Martha a fur coat and some fur-lined boots. 'We'll have to go out the window. The passage is impossible. Hurry!'

'But Dad – What about Dad?' Martha was seizing clothes, struggling into coat and boots. 'Hugh –'

'I'll get him. You first.' Merryck had already pulled on his trousers and was opening the window. An icy blast disturbed the heavy curtains. He leaned out, looking down. It was a cold, bright night, the moon high in the sky, and he was able to see the drop to the snow below. He turned back to Martha. 'What's directly under the window?'

'The patio.'

'Christ! It would be.' Merryck swore. It would take time to knot sheets together, valuable time he couldn't spare if he were to have any hope of rescuing Krasner. 'Okay. I'll let you down as far as I can. Luckily the drop's not bad. Roll with the fall and you'll be all right.'

'And you?'

'I'll jump. But don't wait for me – or anything. Your nearest neighbours – get them to phone the fire brigade and an ambulance. Then call Steve Ross. Understand?'

While he was speaking Merryck was throwing pillows and blankets out of the window to cushion Martha's fall. Martha nodded.

'Come on then,' Merryck said roughly. He helped her out on to the sill. 'I'll hang on to your wrists and lower you. Careful now.'

'What about your hand?'

'Forget it. Hurry, Martha.'

She brushed her lips against his, then concentrated on her escape. Seconds later she was on the ground. Merryck waited only until she'd got to her feet and he was sure she wasn't hurt before he was once more running into the bathroom. This time he turned on both bath taps and the shower, and flung all the available towels under it.

In the bedroom again he seized a sweater and pulled it over his head. He slipped into his shoes, collected the wet towels and threw his hold-all and the towels out of the window. A swift glance round, and he was climbing on to the sill.

Martha had done as he'd said, and run for the nearest house. Her fall had spread out the cushions and pillows and blankets, and Merryck's own landing was heavier than he expected. But he was up immediately, grabbing the towels and hurrying along the side of the building.

Because he had helped Krasner to bed the previous night, he knew that the rooms he occupied – a bedroom with an adjoining bathroom – were at the far corner of the house. Smoke was eddying from the shattered bedroom window, and the snow beneath it was freshly-trodden. Obviously the GDR men had returned sooner than expected, and they had also known where Krasner slept – Martha had been forced to take Karl to the room in search of the memoirs.

Wrapping a towel around his arm, Merryck quickly cleared the rest of the glass from the window frame. Then, a second towel tied round his mouth and nostrils and another over his head, he heaved himself over the sill into a room that at first seemed full of choking smoke. A reeking curtain fell on him as he landed, and he hastily struggled free of its folds.

It was easier to breathe close to the floor, and he could begin to see a little. Luckily there was little actual flame, and the smoke seemed to be coming from smouldering woodwork and furnishings. It was as if the fire, started here with an incendiary grenade of some kind, had moved on through the house, leaving smoking embers behind.

But Krasner? Where was Krasner – or his body? Merryck groped his way across the carpet on hands and knees until he found the bed. Krasner was not in it or near it. Where the hell was the man? It was a big room, impossible to search thoroughly in the time available to him. Already the towels protecting him were starting to dry out and he was beginning to gasp for breath, his chest heaving and aching. He couldn't last in here much longer.

Bathroom. Wet the towels again. That was it! As he stumbled in what he recalled was the direction of the bathroom, a sudden swirl in the grey-blue atmosphere showed him that the door from the bedroom to the corridor and the rest of the house was wide open. Could Krasner have saved himself? Just possibly, Merryck thought. He could have been in his bathroom when the device exploded, for instance. Yes, that door was open too, and there was little to burn in such a fully-tiled interior. Given sufficient presence of mind – which Krasner had already demonstrated in good measure – he could have made it through the bedroom before the flames spread.

Quickly Merryck damped his own all-important towels. He flung them around himself again, and dashed straight through the bedroom smoke to the passage door. In the long corridor the heat was more intense, and there was flame at the end by the burning stairs. Merryck was forced to drop flat on his face. He crawled, seemingly for hours, towards the hall. There, where the air was a trifle clearer, he raised his head and looked around him. Krasner, also face down, but quite still, was lying three feet away, a still-damp towel draped over his head and shoulders.

Merryck didn't hesitate. He inched his way to a position between Krasner and the front door and, as if life-saving in some surrealist swimming pool where the danger of asphyxiation came from smoke above rather than water below, dragged Krasner after him. He had to release the motionless body to rise to his knees and fumble with the chain and lock, but at last he had the door open, and an icy draught blew in.

The cool, clean air gave Merryck strength for a final effort. He grabbed Krasner in his arms, and staggered with him across the wide drive on to the safe, snow-covered lawn. There he fell with his burden. He had no idea whether Krasner was alive or dead, but he could now hear the distant sound of sirens, and he saw figures running towards him. Help was on its way. Krasner was no longer his personal responsibility. Merryck made sure the old man was on his back, his face not buried in the snow. Then, unable to do more, he collapsed beside him.

Merryck could only have lost consciousness for a moment or two. He was aware of the arrival of a station wagon, driven by a tall, thin man accompanied by two strapping teenage boys. Presumably neighbours.

'All out – out of the house?' shouted the man at once.

Merryck roused himself and nodded. 'Kr – Carlton!' he said, pointing. 'He may be gone.'

The big man took in the situation at a glance. Seconds later he was giving Krasner the kiss of life with apparent efficiency. One of the boys was bringing blankets from the station wagon, and the other was offering Merryck brandy from a flask.

'It was there waiting on the hall table,' he said. 'We were ready packed to go up north for a few days. Do some hunting. Get in the wagon if you like. It's warmer and there are more blankets.'

Merryck drank gratefully, and struggled to his feet. Another car appeared – Martha and the neighbour's wife. Then very soon there was the sound of sirens as the professionals arrived – fire service, ambulances, police. An orderly confusion multiplied.

Krasner was quickly moved to an ambulance which sped away, siren blaring. Martha went with it, but before she left she ran to Merryck and kissed him, her eyes full of tears. Her father was alive. Just. Merryck heard someone say, 'Poor Carlton. What a tragedy! Doubt he'll survive.' And, as he walked slowly towards the station wagon, Merryck's mind suddenly focused.

The memoirs! So far Krasner had said nothing useful, except to express his conviction that Francis Dencourt had betrayed Meissener and himself. But this bald statement was no real help. If Krasner died before he could be questioned properly, the memoirs would be the sole source of information. And the only available copy was still in the burning house.

By now the remaining ambulance men had transferred their attention to Merryck. Hastily he waved them away.

'I'll be fine,' he said. 'I look worse than I am. I'll wait here and see it through. Then someone'll give me a lift to the hospital to get cleaned up.'

As they departed Merryck stared gloomily through the wagon's windshield at the firemen playing their hoses on the building. Martha had said the carbon of the memoirs was in her father's study, but where the study was he had no idea. Nor did he know the chances of containing the fire or saving any of the contents of the house. There was nothing he could do, he thought resentfully, but wait. Suddenly he shivered and, looking about, found a rug to pull round his shoulders.

The door beside him opened to reveal a uniformed policeman. 'You okay, sir?' he said. 'You wouldn't go with the ambulance so I guess it's all right to ask you some questions.'

'Sure.' Merryck hid his reluctance, and slid sideways across the seat. The officer got in beside him. Questions were inevitable, but Merryck wished he could have agreed a story with Martha before he had to answer any of them. What was more, he thought, there was that damned hold-all. He certainly didn't want the police poking around in that, and finding Karl's gun.

Merryck gave his name and home address. He said he was a friend of Miss Carlton, and had flown up from New York City with her to spend the weekend with her father. He'd been woken by the smell of smoke, had roused Miss Carlton and they'd escaped from an upstairs window. She'd run for help, and he had gone back into the house in search of Mr Carlton, whom he'd found unconscious in the hall.

'Have you any idea what could have caused the fire, Mr Merryck?'

'None.' It was the first lie Merryck had told. But it wouldn't take the fire service experts long to discover the truth – that an incendiary device had been used. Ross, when he arrived, could cope with that problem.

There were a few more questions, then the police officer said, 'You seem to have been in the wars a bit, Mr Merryck – apart from the fire.'

'Yes.' Merryck was short. He looked down at his filthy bandages. He'd almost forgotten his hands, though now they were hurting intolerably.

'Don't you think you'd better have a check-up?' the policeman persisted. 'We'll run you to the local hospital right away. I'll organize one of our cars.'

Merryck gave in. There was really nothing he could do at the house till morning. Nothing the GDR men could do either; when the authorities had finished they'd certainly leave a guard on the place. And Martha was at the hospital with Krasner. She'd probably know exactly where the type-script was kept.

But there was still the question of the gun. As he climbed out of the station wagon, Merryck called to the boy who had brought him the brandy.

'Would you do something for me?'

'Sure thing. What?'

'I threw a hold-all out of the window at the back of the house. See if you can find it for me. It's pretty big, and it should be on the patio.'

'I'll find it.'

The boy ran off willingly and Merryck, wrapped in his rug, stood outside the police car that had driven up beside him. He wasn't leaving without the bag, and he sought for a plausible explanation.

He said, 'Wait a minute. I must have my bag. It's got everything in it – passport, travellers' cheques – and some clean clothes.' He forced a rueful laugh, and added, 'You're taking me to the same hospital as Mr Carlton and his daughter, aren't you?'

'Sure,' said the driver understandingly. 'North York General. It's not far. And here you are, sir. The boy's got your bag.'

'Thanks a lot,' Merryck said as the boy came up to them. 'I can't tell you how grateful –'

'That's okay.'

Merryck waved him goodbye as the police car shot down

the driveway. He'd meant it when he said he was grateful. He patted the bag on the seat beside him, shut his eyes and tried to relax.

The next moment he was nearly precipitated on to the floor of the back of the car. The police driver shouted sharply. As he was about to turn from the drive on to the road another car had roared up much too fast and, without signalling, made to enter. To avoid a head-on collision both drivers had been forced to jam on their brakes and swerve violently.

The police officer hesitated, swearing under his breath. But no one had been hurt, and the other car was already in motion towards the house. The driver decided not to make an issue of the incident, and contented himself with turning to Merryck.

'That guy needs a ticket,' he said, shaking his head.

'Oh, forget it,' Merryck replied quickly. He too had hesitated for a moment. The other driver had been Steve Ross, presumably reacting to Martha's call. He obviously hadn't seen Merryck in the shadowed rear of the police car, and to return and attempt explanations now would cause endless complications. Ross could readily discover what had happened, and follow them to the hospital.

North York General was modern, and considerably larger than Merryck had expected. But it was not an inner city hospital, so the accident and emergency department was not busy at that time in the early morning. In fact, Merryck was the only patient, but the story of the local fire and his successful rescue had preceded him. He found himself treated as a minor hero by the doctor and nurses on duty – and by Martha, who was awaiting his arrival as he walked through the wide swing doors, the police driver at his elbow. In spite of his filthy state, she hugged him tightly.

'Oh Hugh. How can we ever thank you?'

'No need. How's your father?'

'He's in intensive care. The doctors won't commit themselves, but it was the smoke that laid him out. His heart's okay at the moment. So there's hope.' She did her best to smile.

'Good.' Merryck lowered his voice. 'Ross'll be along soon. Tell him everything that happened, Martha.' He emphasized the word everything. 'And the police'll be asking questions. I told them I was a friend spending the weekend with you. I'd no idea how the fire started.'

As he spoke Merryck looked her straight in the eye. He couldn't be more explicit with a doctor and a nurse beside him, and the policeman at the desk a few yards away. But Martha was highly intelligent and, despite the pre-occupation with her father, immediately grasped his meaning.

She nodded quickly. 'Sure. I understand.'

'Fine. I'll see you soon.'

Martha left him reluctantly, but the doctor was becoming importunate, and Merryck himself appreciated that he needed attention. He was dirty and bedraggled, and his hand and wrist, beneath their tattered bandages, were angry and raw. He guessed he was a wretched sight, and he felt much as he imagined he looked.

Half an hour later, however, showered, in clean pyjamas and robe, his burns treated, his dressings replaced, Merryck was a new man. He didn't want to sleep. He didn't want a sedative. What he really wanted was to talk to Martha again.

But Miss Carlton, he was told, was with her father. Mr Carlton had regained consciousness and had asked for her. It was, the nurse said with a smile, a very hopeful sign.

Merryck returned her smile, and agreed that in that case he might as well rest. He lay on the bed in the small white room to which she brought him, and shut his eyes. He wondered if Ross had reached the hospital yet. Anyway, it was up to Ross to find him . . .

Despite his protestations, Merryck was asleep within minutes. But not for long. Steve Ross had indeed found him. Ross came into the room, and kicked the door shut behind him. Startled, Merryck sat up. Ross stood at the bottom of the bed, his mouth set in a grim line.

'Well?' Ross demanded sharply.

Merryck decided he too could be aggressive. 'What the devil do you mean – well?'

'What happened?'

'Have you seen Martha?'

'Yes, briefly. She seems to think you're God's gift to the Carlton family because you rescued her father just now. What I want to know is what the hell you were doing there anyway – at the Carltons' home.'

'You mean how did I escape from that bloody furnace you left me handcuffed to? And how did I get fifty miles back to Toronto?' Merryck was bitter.

Ross made no answer. He glared at Merryck, who calmly arranged some pillows behind himself. He didn't like Ross, he was never going to like Ross, and the dislike was clearly mutual. But at the moment he needed Ross's co-operation and, what was more, Ross needed his. Merryck felt sure he had at least one bargaining counter to play with – Ross's need to keep the full sensational story out of the media.

Merryck said slowly. 'You'd better sit down, Ross, and listen. First, your chum – Ken Ford – he's dead.'

'What? You killed Ken? You –' Ross, who had sat down in the one chair the room boasted, leapt to his feet threateningly.

'Don't be such a bloody fool!' Merryck said. 'Just be quiet and listen to what I've got to say. I'll tell you exactly what happened – as far as I know it – and we can co-ordinate our stories. I suspect we're going to need to. Or have you got the Canadian authorities in your pocket?'

Ross made no direct answer. Instead he said, 'I'm not co-ordinating a goddam thing with you, Merryck. If you or any of your GDR friends killed Ken Ford, I'll see you pay for it.'

'You can try. But just remember things have changed in the last twelve hours. You've fallen down on your job of protecting Krasner. I've saved his life – twice – and Martha's, as they'll bear witness. Krasner and his daughter are on my side now, Ross. They know they've nothing to fear from me. They know I'm not operating for their enemies.'

'Then who is controlling you?' Ross's anger had cooled a little. 'The Brits? They deny all knowledge of you – and we talked to the people who should know.'

Merryck shrugged. 'So what? You know as well as I do that means nothing. What did you ask them? Did you mentioned Krasner?' Ross didn't answer, and Merryck continued quickly, 'Look, Ross, I appreciate you've got one hell of a security problem with Krasner right now, but all I'm asking is to talk to him – as soon as he's fit enough – about Dencourt. You can be there if you want. He's perfectly willing. Why shouldn't you be?'

'It's a waste of time,' Ross said, a little weakly.

'It's my time.'

'And what do I get in return, Merryck?'

'I can't speak for those GDR hoodlums or their masters, but as far as I'm concerned there'll be no publicity. No screaming headlines about the famous East German defector. No stories about the CIA operating in Canada.' Merryck looked up sharply and saw Ross's eyes flicker; he knew he'd scored a point, and went on. 'Sure I know Krasner could only have been holed up here all these years with Canadian co-operation, but I bet they're pretty sensitive about it. I could spill the whole thing. How would the Agency like that?'

Merryck paused. 'In addition, I'll tell you all I know about the Germans who've been after Krasner – and I'll give you the gun that shot Ford. Is it a bargain, Ross?'

Steve Ross didn't disguise his dislike of the arrangement, but he didn't hesitate either. 'Okay. It's a deal. I'll have to make some long-distance calls, but then you can start talking.'

'Right.'

When Ross returned, Merryck talked. He didn't mention the FCO or Grenley, but maintained that he was acting on behalf of the Dencourt family. Apart from this, he told the truth about his activities in Europe and North America, and answered Ross's questions without prevarication. There seemed no reason to be devious. He certainly owed the GDR men nothing. And Ross's help could be important. After all, there was still the problem of the phoney cab driver whose windpipe he'd destroyed. Merryck hoped that, if the worst came to the worst, Ross or the Agency would think it in their own interests to find some way of squaring the Canadian authorities.

'What do you suppose the Germans'll do with that body?' he asked.

'Easy,' said Ross. He seemed to have at least temporarily forgotten his suspicions of Merryck and was treating him as an equal, almost an ally. 'Obviously the big guy – Karl – didn't want him to be identified, else they'd just have left him. I'd guess he's on his way to being stripped, weighted and sunk in some icy lake. Forget him. There's nothing to connect him with you. Now, where's the gun you say Karl used on Ken?'

'And on Klaus Gerhardt – the chap who stole Krasner's letter from Frau Schmidt in Bonn. Karl admitted it. And a ballistic comparison should prove it.'

'Okay,' said Ross. 'Where's the weapon?'

Still Merryck hesitated. The German's gun was the only piece of hard evidence he possessed – the only thing that, with its fingerprints, would help to clear him. In his judgement, Ross wasn't the kind of man to go back on his word, to produce a double-cross, but –

At this moment there was a knock on the door, and Merryck's dilemma was solved. Martha came in. At once she said, 'Dad's asleep now. He's improving.'

'Fine,' said Merryck. 'Martha, will you remember this? I'm going to give your friend Ross the gun I picked off the floor at your house – the gun that German threatened us with. You saw me take it and put it in my hold-all, didn't you?'

'Yes, I did,' said Martha. 'But why –' She stopped and her eyes widened. She turned to Ross. 'Does this mean you're fool enough to think that Hugh –'

'Never mind, Martha. I'll tell you later,' Merryck interrupted her. 'It's in my bag, Ross, wrapped in a dirty shirt.' He pointed. 'Karl's prints are on it. I handled it by the end of the barrel.'

'Okay,' said Ross. 'Okay.' He looked from Merryck to Martha and back again. 'I'll take care of it.'

Seventeen

Later in the morning, when Martha felt she could leave her father for an hour or two, she and Merryck took a taxi to the house. It was a scene of considerable activity. Cars, including two police vehicles, stood in the drive, and a fire service truck marked 'Salvage' in large letters was parked nearby. The house itself was cordoned off, and a couple of obvious reporters and a camera crew from a local Toronto television station were being kept outside the white tapes, with a group of neighbours who had made an expedition through the snow to inspect the results of the fire. Martha had to identify herself before the two of them were permitted to pass.

The house itself was a sorry sight. The fire, of course, was long out, and there seemed to be no actual structural damage, but smoke and water had wreaked their havoc and the corner that had contained Krasner's suite was blackened and charred. It was here that Martha and Merryck found the worst damage when they were escorted inside by a fire brigade officer. Furnishings were totally ruined, two oils by Emily Carr that had hung in the bedroom were burnt from their frames, glass crunched under foot as they walked among men raking over the debris like scavengers. And throughout the house everything was covered with a thick film of greasy, clinging, black dirt.

'It's dreadful,' Martha said angrily. 'Horrible!' She shivered, and Merryck put an arm round her shoulders and hugged her to him for a moment. 'Damn those Germans! Why should they want to destroy Dad after all these years?'

There was no satisfactory answer that he could give, and Merryck didn't attempt one. Instead he said, 'Look on the bright side, my sweet. They didn't succeed, and the house won't look so bad when it's cleaned up. Most of it's relatively untouched.'

Martha was momentarily distracted from fears for her father. She looked round sadly. 'It's filthy,' she said, 'and it stinks of smoke – the whole place. And why are there so many men around?'

'Police, on guard. You don't want looters to add to everything else, do you? Salvage department men starting to clear things up. Experts to find out exactly how the fire started. Besides, I expect Steve Ross has been in touch with his contacts, and some of these chaps are from the Canadian security service, making sure those GDR characters don't try any more tricks.'

They were back in the main hall by now. Martha was at the closet, reaching down Merryck's car coat which she'd hung there the previous evening. It was undamaged though it, too, smelt of smoke. She turned to him and nodded. 'Sure, I know,' she said. 'I'm being stupid. The house doesn't matter – it's not our home any more. I don't think Steve will ever let Dad come back here to live.'

Merryck said nothing. Obviously she was right, and he wished desperately that he could do something to help. But Ross was in control of the situation now, and he himself was merely an onlooker. He had better think about his own interests, his own operation.

As if to underline his irrelevance to her present problems, Martha said, 'I don't imagine you'll be able to sleep here tonight, Hugh. I'll be staying at the hospital, to be near Dad, but I'm sure one of the neighbours would give you a bed if –'

'No, no. I'll go to an hotel,' Merryck said hurriedly. 'I really only came with you this morning to lend a hand and get my coat and – I was hoping –'

'Hoping? What, Hugh?'

'Martha, if it wasn't burnt, would you lend me that copy of your father's memoirs?' It was a question Merryck had been yearning to ask, but he'd had to choose his moment carefully. 'I don't believe he'd mind my reading it, and it would make it a lot easier to ask him the right questions when he's well enough to talk about Dencourt.'

'Yes. Okay.' Martha's hesitation was minimal. 'I guess he owes you that. It's in a filing cabinet in the study, so it should have been safe enough. But it's the only copy now –'

'I'll take care of it, sweetie. I'll read it this afternoon and give it back to you tonight. We can eat together?'

'Of course, Hugh, if Dad's okay –'

'Fine. Then let's see if we can find it.'

The file of typescript actually in his hands, Merryck felt enormous relief. His main wish now was to get away by himself and read what Krasner had written. He was glad that Martha showed no desire to linger at the house.

At her suggestion he took the rented car, while she drove her father's, and they went in convoy to the nearby Inn on the Park. Luckily the hotel wasn't full, and Merryck was given a room that had been vacated early. As soon as he'd said goodbye to Martha, he went up. He made himself comfortable in an armchair and opened the file on his lap.

Turning the pages rapidly, Merryck found the crucial section, the events that led to Krasner's decision to defect to the West, and the defection itself. He skimmed through it rapidly, and then read it again with complete attention.

Krasner didn't write English easily. His style was stilted and ponderous and only occasionally did he allow his true feelings to show, but some points emerged clearly. Some years after the Communist take-over of East Germany at the end of World War II, Krasner had become disenchanted with much that was happening to his country, and with his own role in it. The so-called German Democratic Republic was a mere province of the USSR, a province to be plundered, so that poverty and destitution were more widespread than in the Soviet Union itself. And always there were the miserable reminders of the power of the one-party state – the secret police *Apparat*, the fear of false accusation, the need to be always on guard, brutality, the barely concealed iron fist.

Krasner, of course, had been in a privileged position. As a

trusted member of the party hierarchy, he had been permitted to travel occasionally to the West, and he knew full well how different conditions were beyond the Curtain. For some years he had kept his mouth shut, playing along with the system and, he claimed, doing what he could to alleviate his country's ills by working from within. But Johann Meissener hadn't seen things that way. He had spoken out with increasing vehemence, uncaring of the danger to himself, and twenty-five or so years ago it had become apparent that, world-renowned philosopher or not, he would end in prison unless he agreed to stay silent and allow his written words to be strictly censored.

For a man such as Meissener there was no choice. His only option was escape – defection – and he had begged his dear friend Otto Krasner to help him, to accompany him, suggesting that they could do more good for their homeland by operating from beyond its borders. Krasner had finally agreed, stipulating only that they should defect to the Americans. Meissener, who remembered Paris and London in the 'twenties and 'thirties, would have preferred to stay in Europe, but Krasner had insisted. He argued that the United States was the centre of the Western alliance, and it was there that they could exert most influence. Their usefulness to Western Intelligence was more likely to be valued at its true worth by United States agencies than by those of Britain, France or even West Germany. Besides, he had never liked the French, it was the British who had killed his first wife and their son in an air raid during the war, and he had little faith in the leaders of the new-born Federal Republic.

Merryck stopped reading. He hadn't known that Krasner had been married before and had a child by that marriage. And the fact that he had refused to defect to the British, despite Meissener's wishes, showed a prejudice that might well have extended to Britain's representative, Francis Dencourt. Perhaps it was a straw in the wind, thought Merryck hopefully, if only a weak one.

Krasner had arranged everything. The details of his initial contact with the Americans were not entirely clear from the typescript. What was clear was that, once they had realized what prizes were being offered them, the United States authorities were prepared to make every effort to smooth the way. A special operation was mounted by the CIA, code-named 'Plato', presumably in honour of Meissener's reputation. Extreme care was taken over security. Only very few senior Agency men were aware of the plan, and none of these was to come under any sort of suspicion after the disaster.

In fact, the plan, as outlined by Krasner, seemed fairly routine, though it did make use of a new and therefore uncompromised crossing-point, held in reserve by the CIA for just such an occasion. The point was west of Heiligenstadt, very close to the boundary between the area of Central Army Group, with its mainly United States forces, and Northern Army Group, commanded by the British. Luckily Meissener had been born in the small town of Mühlhausen, not far away in the Democratic Republic, and it was planned he should visit relations there. For his part, Krasner would pay a semi-official visit to the same place, pick up Meissener and drive to a rendezvous with two Agency men who would guide them across the border.

Because the crossing-point, though uncompromised, was also untried, a contingency plan had been added at the last moment. This involved crossing the border between East and West into the Northern Army Group area. In fact, this plan was not used, but its existence meant that the British had to be informed. Again, security was maintained. Only the British Ambassador in Bonn, Sir Francis Dencourt, knew that the presence of United States Intelligence officers in that area at a particular time was concerned with a defection. Only he knew the identities and importance of the defectors. And, as he was subsequently to admit, at that period Sir Francis had an East German mistress – a refugee, but a refugee who could easily have been under the control of GDR intelligence.

Merryck sighed. He was forced to admit that everything pointed to Dencourt's guilt. Certainly someone had betrayed the plan. The GDR authorities had been there in force, waiting for Meissener and Krasner, the border guards on the alert. It was only due to the extreme courage of one of the Americans – the other had been killed – that Otto Krasner had been brought out safely.

Disappointed, Merryck put down the typescript, got to his feet and stretched himself. The events of yesterday and the short night were catching up with him. He felt stiff and sore, and badly in need of a drink. He rang room service and ordered a light lunch.

It arrived, accompanied by his hold-all that Martha had had the sense to send over from the hospital, and when he'd eaten he started to read Krasner's memoirs through from the beginning. It took him the better part of the afternoon and, as he turned the last page, he was no nearer finding any clue that might point the way to a means of establishing Dencourt's innocence. Unless Krasner came up with something, which now seemed highly unlikely, it looked very much as if Sir Francis Dencourt's name would always be associated with treachery.

This would be a blow for Grenley, Merryck thought regretfully, and for Grenley's superiors. He wondered if it would be a good idea to call London and give some warning of the likely outcome of his mission. But it was late Saturday in London, and Grenley would almost certainly not be immediately available.

Merryck's problem was solved by the phone bell. Martha was on the line. Her father was much improved, his condition stabilized. He'd be happy to see Merryck as soon as he liked.

Merryck arrived at the hospital, Krasner's file under his arm, and at once realized, with relief and grim amusement, that Ross had been in action. Krasner, no longer in need of intensive care, had been moved to a private room. This was located at the end of the corridor, and a desk barred the way to it. Behind the desk, in a white coat, looking the model of a medical orderly, sat John Adamson.

'Mr Merryck.' The man who had escorted Merryck from the main hall spoke softly. Merryck had already decided he was a member of the Canadian security service, or another of Ross's men. 'Okay?'

'Okay. I know Mr Merryck,' Adamson said neutrally.

'Why yes, we spent some time together only yesterday,' Merryck was bland, the irony unstressed.

Adamson ignored the remark. 'You can go right in, Mr Merryck.'

Merryck nodded. 'Thanks.' He tapped at the door Adamson had indicated and went into the room.

Otto Krasner was sitting up in bed, supported by a mass of pillows. Martha sat beside him, holding his hand. And another man in a white coat – presumably a male nurse – was standing by the window.

Krasner's face, so misleading as to his real character, Merryck thought yet again, was slack and grey, but he smiled a welcome. 'Hugh, how kind of you to come.'

It was the first time he'd called Merryck by his Christian name, and Merryck grinned his appreciation. 'It's my pleasure, sir,' he said. He turned to Martha. 'Hello.'

'Hi!' She looked pale and tired, purple bruises under her eyes. She got slowly to her feet. 'I'm going to have a rest while you and Dad talk, Hugh. They've given me the room opposite. Come and fetch me when you're ready.'

'Right.' Merryck opened the door for her, and glanced questioningly from Krasner to the man by the window.

Krasner said, 'Leave us, will you? I'd like to speak with Mr Merryck alone.'

'Yes, sir.' The man didn't question the order, but as he brushed past on his way to the door, Merryck felt the hard bulge beneath his white coat. Ross was taking no chances.

Gesturing towards the chair by his bed, Krasner said, 'Hugh, before anything else, thank you yet again. Not so

183

much for my sake – I shan't have very much longer, and between us I don't greatly regret it, though I'd like to see Lotte's child – but for Martha. If she'd been killed, hurt . . .' He couldn't finish the sentence.

Merryck was a little embarrassed. To give Krasner time to recover, he glanced around the room. Neat and orderly, with the usual accompaniments of illness, it was like a thousand other hosptial rooms. Merryck wondered if Ross had thought to have it bugged.

He said carefully, 'I blame myself for leading your enemies to you. All I can say is I did my best not to.'

Krasner shook his head. 'They'd have found me sooner or later. Once they knew I was alive it was inevitable: they never like a defector to get away unscathed. But the thing I don't understand is why they were so eager to get hold of my memoirs.'

'You know I've read them?' Merryck said. 'In fact, I've got them here, as I promised.'

Krasner nodded. 'Martha told me. No use to you, were they?'

'Not much, unfortunately.'

'I've been thinking about it again – though it was so many years ago it's all very fresh in my memory – and I'd like to help you if I could, Hugh. But if it wasn't Dencourt who betrayed us, who was it?'

'Is it possible Herr Meissener told someone he thought he could trust?'

'No.' It was a flat denial but, reading the scepticism on Merryck's face, Krasner continued. 'Johann has been dead a long time. I've no need to lie to protect him. But Johann and I were told very little, only where to be at a certain date and hour. We couldn't – either of us – have given away the details of the crossing-point. We just didn't know them in advance. The GDR authorities did, however. As we discovered to our cost.'

'What about the Americans?'

'There were only a few, a very few, you know. For instance, the troops in the area were merely told not to patrol along quite a large section of the border for a certain number of hours. That's all. Only a few CIA men knew the details, and they were all grilled afterwards. It was a big enquiry, and the Agency man who was looking after me then swore everyone was clean. They used polygraphs – everything. But they had to leave Dencourt to the Brits. And the sort of in-house enquiry they conducted wasn't very satisfactory, I gather.'

Krasner's voice had sunk to a husky whisper, and Merryck looked at him anxiously. It was obvious the old man had already had enough. There was a thin sheen of sweat on his skin, his breathing was laboured and his fingers plucked nervously at the top sheet. Clearly talking about these old memories had been painful for him.

Merryck said, 'I'm going to leave you now, sir. I hope I haven't tired you too much. Perhaps we could have another chat tomorrow.'

'Of course, though I can't think what more I can tell you. But come anyway. I like to see you.' Krasner smiled wearily.

It was a thoughtful Merryck who collected Martha and took her out to supper. She had chosen a small, intimate restaurant that normally he would have enjoyed. But tonight he had too much on his mind. He was facing the fact that his mission had failed, and there was no reason for him to spend any more of the taxpayers' money on a lost cause.

The failure was not his fault. He couldn't find evidence that didn't exist. Possibly Dencourt was guilty. He wouldn't have been the first Englishman to betray secrets. The FCO would have to accept the situation, and weather the undesirable publicity if some day Krasner's memoirs were published and the old scandal resurrected. At least the British had one card to play: they could pretend dismay at the CIA's concealment of the fact that Krasner had survived.

Colin Grenley, however, was a different matter. Merryck could only hope that Grenley's plan to marry Dencourt's widow wouldn't be affected. He wished, for Grenley's sake, that it could have been otherwise, that he could have exonerated Dencourt. It would have been some repayment, he thought, for Grenley's support during the enquiry over the killing of the hostage.

'Hugh!'

'I'm sorry, darling.' His mind four thousand miles away, Merryck had refilled his own wineglass and ignored Martha's. 'I was thinking.'

'Yes.' Martha smiled. 'Happy thoughts?'

'A mixed bunch.' Merryck poured her wine with unnecessary care, an excuse for not looking at her directly. 'I expect I'll be going back to the UK next week,' he said abruptly. 'I don't think your father can help me much more – and my job's done.'

There was an appreciable pause before Martha spoke. 'Then what, Hugh? Do you stay in London until your Foreign Office sends you off somewhere else?' she asked, overly casual.

'Martha, I don't work for the Foreign Office. Why won't you believe me?' Merryck tried not to sound irritated. 'I wish to hell I did. Once I get home and I'm paid off for this job, I'll be unemployed. Just an ex-soldier looking for work.'

Merryck hadn't meant to be so explicit. Somehow the words had escaped him, and he was only thankful they had come out angrily, without bitterness. He signalled to the waiter for his bill. Martha was playing with the salt and peppers, arranging and rearranging them, and seemed unprepared to say anything. Merryck wished he knew what she was thinking.

As the waiter brought the bill he leant forward and put his hand over hers, stilling her fingers. He said lightly, 'Maybe you'll come over to London one of these days, sweetie, on your way to visit Lotte.'

'Maybe, Hugh.'

Martha withdrew her hand and pushed back her chair. She was wearing a jade green dress that made her eyes seem grey rather than blue, and her face was pale and shadowed. To Hugh Merryck she'd never looked more beautiful. If only, he thought wryly . . . But he wasn't such a fool as not to recognize the impossible.

Hiding his feelings, Merryck tucked his hand under Martha's elbow. 'Let's go,' he said cheerfully.

Merryck dropped Martha at the hospital, and kissed her long and hard before he took the rented car on to his hotel. He was tempted to ask her to come back with him, but he knew it would be a mistake. There was no future in their brief affair, if indeed it was worthy of that name. Much better he should concentrate on his own immediate future, much fairer to Martha . . .

Early the next morning Toronto time he put through a call to London. The usual girl answered, but he was determined to speak to Grenley personally. 'No messages,' he said at once. 'He must call me back. I may need further instructions.'

'Yes, I understand,' she replied. 'If you give me your number, I'll do my best. I don't think there'll be a long delay.'

In the event Colin Grenley rang back within half an hour. He sounded fairly brusque. 'Glad to hear from you, Hugh. What news?'

'A lot's been happening. The Company tried hard — violently — to stop me, but I managed to trace our friend. In fact, I spent a night in his house.' The good news first, Merryck thought. 'He's been as co-operative as he could.'

'Meaning?' Grenley asked.

'Our chums from the other side of the wall intervened, with the result he's now in hospital.'

'How bad?'

'All right, eventually. Actually he's weathered the last twenty-four hours pretty well, I'd say, considering his dicky heart.'

Grenley grunted. 'And you've talked to him?'

'Yes, a fair amount, Colin. And I've read his memoirs with the greatest care.' Merryck paused, half hoping for a word of commendation. 'No go, I hate to say. He firmly believes in the accepted story, and as far as I can see there's absolutely nothing to prove him wrong.'

'You're certain?'

'I expect to have another chat with him tomorrow, but I'm as sure as anyone can be. I'm sorry, Colin.'

'That's a pity, Hugh – a great pity. Some hard evidence would have solved a lot of problems. But I suppose it always was a bit of a long shot. We'll talk about it when I see you.'

'In a couple of days, I expect.'

'Fine,' said Grenley. 'Incidentally, you're all right, aren't you? No – problems? You implied there'd been some trouble.'

'No problems that haven't been resolved.'

'Okay,' Grenley said. 'Phone as soon as you get to Heathrow. And there's just one other thing. You mentioned the Company. I imagine it'll be their policy to arrange a trip somewhere for our friend – a long convalesence, let's say. If you could find out where, Hugh, it might be useful for the record.'

'Yes. Of course. I'll try.'

An hour later, Martha called. Her father had died in his sleep. Once more Merryck reached for the phone and dialled London.

Part IV

OUTCOME

Eighteen

Decked in her spring finery, the sun shining in a soft blue sky, London was looking her best this Tuesday morning. As Colin Grenley walked briskly through St James's Park on his way to his club he thought how much he loved the city, how much he would miss it. Others could have Paris, Rome, New York, Bangkok. As far as he was concerned, there was no place like London.

But Washington? That was a plum he couldn't refuse – not perhaps for its attractions as a place to live, but for a variety of other reasons. Of course it hadn't been offered yet, not officially, and no doubt others had also been sounded out. But there couldn't be many on the short list, and from what the Foreign Secretary had murmured last night at Julia's, it seemed probable that the plum would be there for the picking.

Grenley hummed to himself as he strode along. Apart from the chance of an excellent posting, there was a lot going for him at the moment. His mother had been reasonably amenable in recent weeks, and his daughter had found herself a new boy-friend, someone quite presentable, someone he could approve of.

Then there was Julia. She was a wonderful hostess, and together – what a pair they'd make in Washington when she'd married him. Julia – witty, charming, influential and marvellous in bed; Colin Grenley recalled the previous night with pleasure.

Of course, the Krasner case was still unfinished. Grenley stopped humming. There could be trouble over that, real trouble. But he'd be in a better position to judge the possibilities when he'd talked to Hugh Merryck.

Grenley ran up the steps of his club and swung through the door. He said good morning to the hall porter, and asked if Merryck had arrived.

'Yes, sir, five minutes ago. I put him in the smoking-room, as you said.'

'Thanks.' Grenley hurried along to the smoking-room. Merryck rose as he came in, and Grenley saw the bandaged hands and the tired eyes. Grenley said, 'You must have had quite a time, Hugh. It was good of you to get in touch immediately you landed, but I'm glad you did. It's important we should know the whole story as soon as possible.' He paused to order drinks, then said abruptly, 'First, Hugh, you're certain Krasner's dead this time? There's no chance the CIA are pulling another fast one?'

Merryck was slightly surprised at this choice of initial question, but he responded positively. 'None whatsoever,' he said. 'Krasner died early on Sunday morning. I saw the body.' He stopped for a moment, remembering Martha's grief, then went on. 'Conveniently, it was natural causes in the end. There'll be a post mortem, of course, but there's no doubt it was his heart – the excitement of the fire on top of everything else; it was only to be expected.'

Grenley frowned. 'Conveniently? In the end? How do you mean?'

'It's like this, Colin. The whole affair's being hushed up over there. They've put a tight clamp on everything – the two attacks on Krasner before he died, the cause of the fire, everything. The fact that he did eventually die naturally makes it all much simpler. A chap called Carlton, a respected Toronto citizen, who suffered from a heart condition, had a fatal attack after a fire at his home. He had no connection with any East German politician called Krasner. That's the way the CIA want it. That's the way the Canadians want it. That's the way the family want it.' Merryck fidgeted with his glass, uncertain of Grenley's reaction to what he was about to say. 'And I made a kind of commitment on your behalf.'

'On my behalf?' Grenley was sharp.

'Well – on behalf of a non-existent member of the Den-court family who I swore I was working for. It's all right, Colin, I didn't break my cover, such as it was. And I didn't involve the FCO, though the Langley boys have got their suspicions.'

'And the commitment?'

'That the Dencourts will go along with them – no publi-city, no scandal. Preferably not even a rumour. I was sure the Dencourts – and you – would agree.'

'Why not?' To Merryck's relief, Grenley raised no objec-tion. Instead, he made an expansive gesture. 'If we can't clear Francis Dencourt – and it seems we can't – there's no point in raking over old coals. But what about Krasner's memoirs?' he asked suddenly. 'Suppose they leak?'

'Martha Carlton, the elder daughter, has agreed they shouldn't be published, and her copy's in the hands of the Agency. She doesn't want any publicity, as I said, and nor does her sister Lotte – the one in Paris. Of course, the GDR authorities have got a copy, and there's no way of knowing what they might do with it. But Ross – he was the Langley man in charge – seemed to think they'll avoid publishing anything that might show how they've been hoodwinked all these years.'

'He may well be right.' Grenley finished his drink and put down the glass. 'That's fine then. You seem to have done a good job, Hugh. It's a pity you couldn't help to prove Dencourt's innocence, but one can't expect miracles.' He glanced at his watch and got to his feet. 'Let's go and eat, and you can tell me everything from the beginning.'

Over lunch Merryck recounted at length the details of his search for Otto Krasner, and its outcome. The only point he glossed over was his relationship with Martha Carlton, and Grenley, whatever he guessed, tactfully asked very few questions about her.

'So that's it,' Merryck said as he reached the end. 'And many thanks for the job, Colin.'

'Thank you for taking it on,' Grenley replied. 'I must admit when I suggested it I had no idea it would prove dangerous. But you've done well, Hugh. As much as anyone could have done.' He nodded at Merryck's bandages. 'I hope your hands are improving.'

'They're fine, Colin. They don't give me any trouble now.'

'Good.'

Grenley turned to practicalities – pay, expenses and so on. But he made no mention of further assignments or of any kind of permanent employment. It was left to Merryck to raise the question tentatively, and Grenley's response, though sympathetic, was unencouraging. 'I know your position, Hugh,' he said, 'but jobs aren't so easy to find. However, tell me where you're staying in London, and maybe I'll come up with something.'

Merryck thanked him as they parted on the steps of the club. At least money wasn't a problem for the moment, he thought. But it wouldn't last for ever, and if he couldn't find some means of earning a living within a reasonable time, he'd be back in the Isle of Wight, without purpose, cadging off his parents again.

Loath to return immediately to the rather dreary bedsitting-room in Marylebone that he'd found for himself during the morning, Merryck dawdled his way northwards through St James's Square and up to Piccadilly. He spent half an hour in Hatchards without buying even a paperback, but as he was leaving he noticed a new book on military history, and remembered his father's forthcoming birthday.

Clutching the bookshop's distinctive black plastic carrier bag, Merryck came out of the store into the afternoon sunshine, to the roar of traffic and the smell of diesel fumes. He'd drunk a lot of wine at lunch, far more than his share, and he had an incipient headache. He stood at the edge of the kerb with a knot of other people waiting to cross the road, their heads turned to watch an approaching bus.

The bus wasn't far from them now, a bright red lumbering monster, safe in its own private lane from the rest of the traffic that streamed in the opposite direction towards Piccadilly Circus. Merryck saw the driver sitting high, his eyes on the road ahead, concentrated on his job. Instinctively, like those around him, Merryck drew back a little. Then someone gave him a punching blow in the small of the back.

The attack was wholly unexpected, and there was nothing Merryck could do to save himself. Arms flailing, he was flung forward under the wheels of the bus. The surface of the road came up and hit him. And he lay, eyes tight shut, cringeing, already feeling his bones splintering as the great weight of the vehicle passed over him. It was a long, agonizing instant of time.

Seconds later Merryck opened his eyes, slowly, apprehensively. He could see a wide black rubber tyre within inches of his face. He could feel waves of heat from the stalled engine. By some miracle, or so it seemed to Merryck at that moment, the driver had managed to stop his bus.

Merryck lay in the road, temporarily paralysed with shock. Somewhere close by a woman was screaming. Then anxious hands reached out to lift him, and he found that he could struggle to his feet, shaking. People clustered around, asking questions, brushing him down. A couple of police officers had appeared, and the bus driver was busy denying all responsibility.

One of the officers took Merryck by the arm. 'Are you all right, sir? Do you want to go to hospital?'

Merryck gritted his teeth. He was getting control of his shakes. 'No. I'm okay. I'm sorry. I must have slipped or something.' He waited for somone to contradict him, but no one spoke. 'It certainly wasn't the bus driver's fault. In fact, I owe him. If his reactions hadn't been so quick –'

The driver, mollified by the praise, grinned at Merryck. 'Cor, guv! I thought you was a goner when you leapt out under my wheels.'

The police officer looked at Merryck sharply, curiously,

taking in his bandaged hands, sensing his air of fatigue and despondency. 'I'll radio for a car to take you home, sir,' he said, holding out the black plastic bag that someone had found in the gutter.

'No need.' Guessing what was in the policeman's mind, Merryck spoke decisively. 'I'm fine. It was just a silly accident. No harm done.' He took the carrier bag and opened it. The book he had just bought was bent and squashed. For a moment he steadied himself on the bus as he thought of what might have happened.

'All the same, I think perhaps, sir –'

'Hugh!' A man with reddish hair and bright, intelligent eyes was pushing his way through the group of bystanders that had gathered at the scene. 'I couldn't get across before. I was the other side of the road, and the lights were against me. Are you okay?'

Merryck ignored the question, but his grin couldn't have been more welcoming. Ian Hume was an old friend. They had been at school and Sandhurst together, and had kept in touch ever since. Now Hume was solving Merryck's immediate problem. He turned to the policeman.

'Thanks for the offer,' he said, 'but you can see I don't need any help. I'm with a friend.'

As the pubs were not yet open Hume suggested tea, and they went along to Simpsons basement. Seated together at a small corner table, Merryck was aware of Hume's enquiring gaze, and conscious of his bandaged hands. Some explanations would be needed, but for a while the conversation was casual, an exchange of news and gossip.

Then Hume said, 'Were the police being difficult, Hugh?'

'Just now?' Merryck did his best to sound unconcerned. 'Not really. Over-zealous, perhaps. They wanted to take me home. I think they suspected I'd jumped under the bloody bus on purpose.'

'Silly buggers.' Ian Hume laughed. He poured himself a second cup of tea, added milk and stirred it thoughtfully.

Without looking up, he said, 'Why is someone trying to kill you, Hugh?'

Merryck was suddenly cold. Ever since the incident he had been persuading himself it was accidental. What he had felt as a punch in the back had probably been someone's elbow or the corner of a shopping-bag. Any other suggestion was absurd. Otto Krasner was dead and buried. The file was closed. The GDR authorities had achieved their aim. They weren't going to pursue him to London merely to avenge an agent, the so-called cab-driver he'd killed in Toronto. And anyway they'd had plenty of opportunities in Canada. If they'd wanted him dead, why hadn't they killed him there?

Deliberately he raised his cup to his mouth and drank. Then he said, 'My dear chap, you're imagining things! Who on earth would want to kill me?'

'That's what I'm asking you.'

'The answer's no one, of course. For heaven's sake, Ian! You'd better get back to some plain regimental soldiering and forget your Intelligence jobs. You've been leading too exciting a life. Your imagination's working overtime.'

Hume didn't respond to this banter. He said quietly, 'I saw you outside Hatchards, and I was going to come across to you when the lights changed. Hugh, I was waving, trying to attract your attention, so naturally I was watching. There were several people round you, but one guy came up right behind you just before the bus reached the spot – and either he shoved you or you decided you'd had enough of this life. Because you didn't fall – I'm certain of that. You positively dived in front of those wheels.'

'What was he like, this chap? And where did he go?' Merryck did his best to sound amused.

Hume took the questions seriously. 'The bus hid him from my view almost immediately, and by the time I'd got across the road he'd disappeared. He certainly didn't hang around to see what happened. A biggish man, powerful-looking, wearing one of those brown duffel coats that used to be so popular.'

Hume was watching him closely, and Merryck tried hard not to react. He attempted to convey disbelief, disinterest, but he knew he'd failed. Hume had described Karl, the East German, with fair accuracy, and the coincidence was surely too great to be ignored. All the same, it was absurd . . .

'Means nothing to me,' Merryck lied flatly. 'I'd have thought it a bit warm for a duffel coat today.'

'Perhaps he's a cold-blooded character. Anyway, it's your funeral, but I'd keep a sharp look out behind me for a while.' Hume waited a moment. 'You say you've just come from Toronto. Could this chap have anything to do with what you were up to over there?'

This was the question Merryck had been waiting for. 'Of course not,' he said, and went on to give a brief, edited account of his activities. He was annoyed at having to lie to Ian, but it was impossible to tell him the truth. As soon as he could, he looked at his watch. 'Ian, I must go. It was good to see you. And thanks a lot for being around when you were needed.'

Hume didn't argue. 'Forget it,' he said. 'I must go too. I should have been back in the office hours ago. But let's make a date. What about coming round to my flat for a meal one night this week?'

'Great! Any night you like.'

'Make it Thursday?'

'Fine.'

Having arranged to meet, they went their separate ways, Merryck to Piccadilly Circus to catch a bus. On the way he dropped his book into a litter-bin. His father wouldn't appreciate a battered copy as a birthday present. And even less, thought Merryck grimly, would he like a battered, murdered son.

Ian Hume returned to his office in a nondescript block near Victoria Station. His thoughts were not dissimilar to Merryck's, and he immediately requested a meeting with his boss.

'Sir, by the merest chance I've just met Hugh Merryck,' he began. 'You remember –'

'Of course.' General Sir Claud Bothwell raised a shaggy eyebrow. 'He's back in the UK then?'

'Yes. He flew in this morning from Toronto.'

'Did he say what he'd been doing there?'

'He told me he'd been tracing someone who'd emigrated to North America some years ago. He wasn't very forthcoming, but he did admit he'd been successful. And he seems to have made some enemies.'

'We know that, or we can guess it.' The General was impatient. 'The CIA wouldn't have been enquiring about him if he hadn't been getting in their hair. They said as much.'

'No. Not the Agency, sir – someone else is gunning for him. Merryck was nearly killed this afternoon. I saw a man push him under a bus, and that's not the CIA's style. Only the incredibly quick reaction of the bus driver saved him.'

'You saw this! Why the hell didn't you say so before?'

Hume refrained from saying he'd had no chance. He explained exactly what he'd witnessed in Piccadilly, and gave an almost verbatim account of his chat with Merryck over tea. He concluded by commenting, 'Merryck denied it, but I swear he recognized my description of the man who shoved him.'

The General disentangled his legs from under his desk and started to pace up and down his office. 'Let's try to get the facts straight, Ian. According to the Agency, who wanted to know if we were behind him. Merryck's been making enquiries about that old Dencourt business. Merryck himself says he's been tracing someone who went to Canada a while ago. Merryck could be lying –'

'I don't think so, sir. Not about that. He seemed to be choosing his words very carefully. I think he wanted to avoid a direct lie.'

'If you're right, we can assume a connection between Dencourt and an emigrant. But where does the CIA come in?

Suppose the emigrant – immigrant – turned out to be an agent – that would involve the security services – or even a defector . . .'

The General's voice trailed away. He stopped pacing and stood, his back to Hume, staring out of the window to the street below. It was the beginning of the rush hour. Traffic was already dense. Pedestrians scurried along the pavements or queued for transport. A barrow boy was packing up his wares. A news vendor was shouting the headlines of the latest edition of the *Standard*. The General regarded the scene almost benevolently. Softly he said, as if to himself, 'No. It can't be. Surely not.'

But as he swung round to Ian Hume, his eyes were bright, his handsome face alight with excitement. 'I've just had a wild idea, Ian.'

Hume grinned. He was accustomed to the General's wild ideas. Often they fizzled out like damp squibs, but sometimes they were flashes of genius. In either case they were worth considering.

'Can you get hold of young Merryck?' asked the General.

'Not very easily, sir. I gather he's in a bed-sit in Marylebone. There's a payphone in the hall, but no guarantee a message'll be delivered. However, if it would wait, sir, he's having dinner with me the day after tomorrow.'

'Splendid! That'll give us time to make a few enquiries. I think I'll start with Colin Grenley. If the East German Desk has set up some mission of their own without consulting us, he's the man most likely to know. And it's far from impossible.'

Nineteen

It was a shabby room, the carpet worn, the furniture disfigured with burn marks, the elements in the gas fire broken. To Merryck, adjusting himself to the uncomfortable springs of the single armchair, it was incredibly depressing. He yawned. The evening was still young, but he felt tired and dispirited.

The night before he'd slept badly, tossing and turning, the lumpy mattress no help, dreaming of a burly man in a duffel coat. And today had been little better. He had been tempted to find somewhere more pleasant to live while he was in London, but told himself it was important to save money. He'd made no progress towards finding a job. And, in spite of brooding about it, he still remained unsure whether the bus incident had really been an attempt on his life. He'd decided to take no action, let things slide and see what happened.

Angry with himself at this evidence of lack of initiative, Merryck stood up and stretched. He'd go round to the Red Fox, a pub a few streets away that he'd once known well. Maybe he'd meet an old chum and they could get drunk together.

It was more than two years since he'd been in the Red Fox, and much longer than that since he'd been a regular, but the place hadn't changed. The same hunting prints were on the walls, and the fox's brush still over the bar. He saw no one he knew, but it was a friendly pub, warm and companionable, and Merryck was well content.

About nine o'clock a girl came in. She was tall and very thin, with the flat, narrow body of a model, straight black hair and grey eyes. In a pub where most people were wearing jeans and sandals, her fake ermine jacket over a long orange-coloured dress drew Merryck's attention. He frowned. The girl looked familiar, but he couldn't place her.

Suddenly her eyes met his and, smiling, she came across the room to him, hand outstretched. 'Hugh! It's Hugh Merryck, isn't it?' She had a low, throaty voice. 'Don't you remember me? Diana Grey.'

Merryck made room for her beside him on the window-seat. 'Yes, of course.' It was true. He did remember her. She'd been a singer of some kind. 'How's the music business?'

She wrinkled her nose. 'Not good. I drink too much. So I'm not reliable and mostly I'm resting. How's the soldiering?'

Merryck grinned. 'Much the same as your singing. I got out.' He made to stand up. 'Let me buy you a drink.'

She laid a hand on his arm. 'I come in here most nights,' she said, 'just for a bit of company, but I've liquor at home. Why not come back with me? Have you eaten? I'll make you an omelette. I'm a pretty good cook.'

Merryck had no doubt what she was offering. He guessed she was in the habit of picking men up in the pub, but he didn't mind. She was an attractive girl and obviously lonely, and he'd no desire to return to his miserable bed-sitter before he had to.

'Why not?' he said. 'Let's go.'

Diana Grey hadn't been boasting when she said she was a good cook. She produced an excellent late supper for them, and when predictably they ended in bed, Merryck enjoyed that too.

He slept well, waking only once, around three in the morning. Something had disturbed him, and for a few moments he listened hard. He heard sirens, but they were in the distance and coming no closer. He turned on his side and was soon asleep again.

When he woke much later, the brief gap between dreams forgotten, he made himself some breakfast and said goodbye to Diana. Still half asleep, she scarcely noticed his departure.

Then, thinking of the day that stretched ahead and the evening he was spending with Ian Hume, he set off back to his room.

He was turning the corner at the end of his street when he saw the barriers and the white tapes. Further down the road were a couple of fire engines, police cars, a group of officials. Some workmen and a small bulldozer were standing by. Merryck's mouth went suddenly dry and he ran his tongue over his lips.

'What happened?' he said to the policeman at the barrier.

'We're not sure yet, sir.' The officer was surprisingly forthcoming. 'Neighbours say there was a great bang. Just like one of those V-bombs in the last war, according to one bloke. They think it might have been a gas leak, but I don't know. Maybe some terrorist blew himself up.' He shrugged his shoulders.

Merryck stared at the space that the evening before had been a house. Now all that remained were a few walls, a bed tilted at an obscene angle, a picture hanging crazily from a nail. He tried to visualize the position of the room he should have been occupying, but it had ceased to exist.

'Many hurt?'

'Eight dead. Some others badly injured,' said the policeman. 'And there may be some still buried in the mess. There's no way of knowing how many people were staying in that sort of rooming-house.'

Merryck turned away quickly. He'd seen enough. He felt physically sick and no longer had any doubts; the coincidence was too great. But the first attempt on his life in London had threatened only one person – himself. This was quite different – eight dead, perhaps more. There had to be a very serious reason to justify such an attack.

Merryck walked rapidly, his mind seething. He was amazed that the East Germans had struck again so quickly, though perhaps he should have been expecting it; after all, it was precisely what they'd done to Otto Krasner. But here, ·on his home ground . . .

And a third attempt – was that in the cards? Almost certainly, if they knew they'd failed. They could have kept the house under observation and seen him return to it – or what remained of it. He couldn't count on being safe, even for a short time. He was going to need help. He couldn't take on an entire bloody foreign agency by himself.

By now he was in Marylebone High Street, and he went into the Post Office to find a phone-box that hadn't been vandalized. He dialled the now familiar number, and waited.

The usual girl answered on the fourth double ring. She sounded slightly breathless and gave her number, rather than announcing 'Mr Grenley's office'. But she recognized Merryck's voice at once, and agreed to take an urgent message.

'It's vital he gets it in the course of the day,' said Merryck. 'Tell him this. Tell him I've had a couple of bits of trouble – unpleasant trouble – since I left him yesterday. Tell him I'm going to drop out of sight for the rest of the day, but he can reach me after eight this evening at –' He gave Ian Hume's name and phone number. 'Emphasize it's urgent and important.'

'I've got all that, Mr Merryck,' said the girl. 'I'll certainly be able to get hold of him this afternoon. But is there anything I can do in the meantime?'

For a moment Merryck hesitated. Then he thought, the hell with it! I can do better on my own till I've talked to Grenley. 'No,' he said. 'Just make sure Mr Grenley gets in touch.'

He came out of the Post Office, walked across to Baker Street and swung onto a passing bus just as it was picking up speed. The most pressing thing now was to shake any tail he might have acquired, and surely here in a city he knew so well he had an advantage over Karl and his chums. He must buy himself a few clothes, too – he had nothing but what he was wearing – and make sure that he arrived on Ian Hume's doorstep at eight that evening, unharmed and unaccompanied.

Merryck achieved this without difficulty, to be greeted by Ian Hume, who said quickly, 'Come in and welcome, but don't relax yet. I've a message for you, Hugh.'

'Yes?' Merryck put down his brand new overnight bag and gave Hume the bottle of wine he'd brought as a gift.

'Thanks.' Hume grinned. 'It's Colin Grenley of the Foreign Office. He wants you to ring him – something about a job, I gather. There's the phone, and his home number's on the pad. Better be quick. He's going out to dinner. He seemed to know you'd be coming here and he's waiting for you to call.'

'Yes,' said Merryck. 'I took the liberty of giving him your number. I was sure you wouldn't mind. He sat down on the stool beside the hall telephone and dialled. Colin Grenley answered almost at once. 'Oh, Hugh. Good! Now, listen. I suspect you can't speak freely where you are, but I think I know what you want to say. Will you be all right for another twenty-four hours? Answer yes or no.'

'I guess so,' said Merryck. 'If –'

'Good. Then come round to my house – 29 Crockford Square – at six-thirty tomorrow. We'll have a drink and go into the situation thoroughly.'

'All right. I'll do that, but –'

'And Hugh, the message I left with Hume wasn't entirely false. I think we may have found something more permanent for you. We can discuss that too. In any case, that's what Hume must think we're talking about now, and that's the ostensible reason we're meeting tomorrow. Be careful what you say to Hume. He'll be curious, and he's shrewd. His boss has already been asking questions. Whatever you do, don't mention me in connection with your last assignment, will you? That's vital. You know what Whitehall's like. I can depend on you?'

'Of course.'

'Good. Till tomorrow then.'

Thoughtfully Merryck put down the receiver. He should have felt cock-a-hoop at the prospect of a job. Instead, he had a vague sense of disquiet. He wished Grenley hadn't been so emphatic about the need to keep his mouth shut. Shrugging his shoulders, he went into Hume's sitting-room.

'Whisky? Gin? Most other things?' Hume enquired cheer-fully.

'Whisky, please.'

'We're going to eat at nine, which gives us lots of time to talk, Hugh, and we've got a lot to talk about, I suspect. So we need a drink – probably several. Incidentally, I see you brought a bag. Are you spending the night here?'

'I'd be awfully grateful.'

'Fine. I was expecting you. The guest room's all ready – and there's no gas in the building so we won't get blown up that way.'

Merryck looked at him in surprise. 'How on earth –'

'Quite simple. The explosion was mentioned on the news and in the evening paper. And you'd told me where you were staying. After what happened in Piccadilly yesterday it didn't take a genius to put two and two together. In fact, I feared the worst, till I'd made a few enquiries. But I was still glad when you turned up tonight, Hugh.'

'Thanks.' Merryck took a long pull at the drink Hume had given him.

'Now, I've got something to tell you. My boss, General Bothwell, thought it might have been the FCO who'd sent you off to North America to trace this chap called Krasner – Otto Krasner.' Hume looked up suddenly at Merryck. 'Krasner was an East German defector – a GDR politician who made an attempt to come across about twenty-five years ago. We thought he was dead.'

Merryck found it difficult to hide his surprise and dismay. 'Christ! How did –'

'How did the General know anything about you and Krasner? Partly from some queries we've had from the CIA. Partly from what you told me at tea yesterday. And partly from some inspired guesswork, putting together a few odd items of information from other sources.' Hume regarded

Merryck with some sympathy. 'Anyway, the General phoned Colin Grenley about you – quite off the record. Grenley always knows what's going on in the FCO, though he doesn't always tell. But Grenley said he didn't know a thing.'

Merryck finished his whisky and put down his glass. He had his feelings under control by now, and was remembering Grenley's warning. He remarked with apparent unconcern. 'Of course Colin denied all knowledge of my activities. All he's trying to do is find me a job, and he may have succeeded. That's why he wanted me to call him. We've got a date tomorrow evening at his house. As for the other business you and your General seem to know so much about – it's true I was looking for Krasner, but I was working for the Dencourt family, not the FCO.'

'I see,' said Hume sceptically.

Merryck hesitated. Hume knew so much already that it was pointless to lie to him unnecessarily. So, apart from substituting a mythical Dencourt for Colin Grenley, he gave Hume a full account of his travels and his search. Tomorrow night he'd have a chance to warn Grenley of the line he'd been forced to take.

'Ian,' he concluded, 'I'm quite prepared to accept that the GDR authorities are still after me, but I can't work out why. I don't believe it's because I could identify some of their hoods if I met them again, nor because I killed one of them, nor because Krasner might have told me something about Dencourt. None of this seems important enough to make them mount operations like this in London. And, what's more, I keep telling myself they could easily have killed me in Toronto if they'd really wanted to.'

They were still mulling over the problem when they went into the dining-room. The telephone rang as they were sitting down. Hume swore. 'Go ahead, Hugh. I'll be with you in a minute.'

It was a fish soup, and very hot. Merryck sipped it slowly, but he'd finished it and still Hume hadn't returned. He sat, waiting. The call must be important to delay Hume for so long. He wondered if Hume had been expecting it; he hadn't taken it in the hall, but had gone along to his bedroom and shut the door. Merryck couldn't even hear the murmur of his voice.

By the time Hume finally returned to the dining-room his soup was quite cold. He carried it out to the kitchen without comment. He seemed a little distrait, and after he'd served the main course he said suddenly, 'I hope you don't mind, Hugh. The General's coming round in half an hour or so. He'd like to talk to you himself.'

'Ian, I don't want –'

'I tried to put him off, but no go. Not after I told him how you'd filled me in on your story.' Hume grinned wryly. 'The General's a forceful man, and he is my boss. I'm sorry.'

Merryck felt himself to be under pressure, and resented it. But there was little he could do. 'Okay, if I must,' he said reluctantly. 'I didn't bargain on some sort of official interrogation, but maybe he can help, think of some new angle.'

General Bothwell, when he arrived, had much the same idea. 'What we need,' he said firmly, accepting a cup of coffee and a brandy, 'is a completely different approach. First of all, Merryck, how well do you know this Dencourt relative who commissioned you to take this job?'

'I –' Merryck was startled by the question. 'Scarcely at all.'

'He must be a rich man if he was prepared to pay you to travel all over the place in the vague hope you might discover something to clear the name of a long-dead relative.' The General made the proposition sound absurd. 'Merryck, has it occurred to you that his true purpose was to locate Krasner so that the East Germans could kill him?'

'No. You're – you're saying he was working for them, sir, and that's ridiculous.'

'It's not in the least ridiculous. It's a possibility to consider. I think the GDR authorities tried to follow up the letter Krasner wrote his sister and failed. So you were employed, an Englishman, a new face, not on anyone's active files – just the sort of fellow all services have to use occasionally. And you had a very sympathetic line about Francis Dencourt. All the GDR had to do was follow you. I imagine that wasn't too difficult if you kept your – employer informed of your movements. You did, didn't you?'

'Yes, mostly.' Merryck replied automatically to the abrupt question.

'Well, that explains how they were a jump ahead of you so often. For instance, they didn't mind being shaken in New York, for they knew you'd be flying into Toronto. They were prepared to risk losing you after they'd rescued you from that cottage; after all, you might not have taken the cab they planted. But all they had to do was wait for another phone call.' The General paused for Merryck to comment, but when he remained silent said, 'Tell me how you were approached in the first place, Merryck.'

Silently cursing the false position he was in, Merryck had to elaborate his story. He said he'd been telephoned in the Isle of Wight. Apparently a mutual acquaintance – un-named – had known Merryck was desperately seeking work, and had recommended him. There had been two or three meetings in London restaurants to discuss the job and the details. That was all.

'And during the operation you kept in touch by phone?'

'Yes.' It was a reluctant admission. Merryck could see where the question was leading, but he couldn't avoid it.

'And what was the phone number?'

'The number?' Merryck pretended to think. '930? No, that wasn't it. 935? I'm sorry, sir, I really can't remember.' Out of the corner of his eye he saw Ian Hume shake his head in disgust at such a weak and obvious prevarication.

'As you wish,' General Bothwell said, 'but I'd advise you to try to recall it. Because it may interest you to know that no single member of the Dencourt family seems to have heard of you. Merryck, whatever he may have called himself, the man you were working for was not a Dencourt.'

The General leant forward in his chair and looked Merryck straight in the eyes. 'I have a theory. You see, I knew Francis Dencourt. He was a dreadful womanizer, couldn't keep his hands off the girls. But I'm one of those who never believed he was a traitor – I still don't – and I think it conceivable the GDR wanted Krasner dead in case, even unknowingly, he might provide a clue to the real villain. And that means the traitor could be an agent still in place.'

The General sat back slowly. 'It's only a theory, Merryck, but I suggest you give it some thought – some hard thought.'

He stood up abruptly. 'Ian knows how to contact me,' he said.

Twenty

Shortly before six the following morning Hugh Merryck quietly let himself out of Ian Hume's flat. He avoided the lift and ran down the stairs. The hall of the building was empty, the porter nowhere to be seen, and Merryck was able to open the main door unobserved. It was that indeterminate time between night and day. The street lamps were still on, the streets themselves practically deserted.

Merryck walked briskly. Because there were so few people about it was easy for him to make sure he wasn't being followed. He kept his eyes open for an early taxi, but with no luck. Eventually he settled for the tube, which took him to Waterloo Station. Here he bought a ticket for Ryde, in the Isle of Wight. Where it had all started, he thought wryly.

With twenty minutes to spare he breakfasted off a pot of tea and some soggy toast in a station buffet, and then found a corner seat in the almost empty train. He settled himself as comfortably as possible, intending to doze his way to Portsmouth Harbour. He had no plans to make. He'd done his thinking the night before, and knew what action he must take.

Merryck had just time to telephone his home from the Harbour Station. His mother was delighted to hear from him, and she and his father would meet the next hovercraft. He waited till they were all in the car to break the news that he must be back in London the same night.

'Oh, Hugh!' His mother was disappointed. 'Can't you stay over the weekend? It's your father's birthday on –'

'I know, but it's impossible, I'm afraid.'

'Is it this new job of yours?' the Brigadier asked. 'Going all right, then?'

'Yes. It's fine.' Merryck disliked lying to his parents, but there seemed no alternative. He parried his father's questions and said, 'I may be sent abroad for a while, so I decided to come down and pick up a few things.'

In fact, there was only one item that Merryck had come for. As soon as he had the chance he went to his bedroom, unlocked the bottom drawer of his desk and took out a packet wrapped in an old shirt and a plastic bag.

He spent half an hour carefully cleaning the Makarov pistol. It was a reminder of certain weeks in the Middle East, and was of course a totally illegal possession in the UK. He had almost unwittingly brought it into the country in his baggage while he was an SAS officer. The 9 mm ammunition was standard.

Finally satisfied with the pistol, he loaded it, telling himself he didn't really expect to have to use it. It was merely an insurance policy. But he knew he would feel considerably more secure with it to hand.

There was maintenance work on the line, and the train from Portsmouth was twenty minutes late arriving at Waterloo. Taxis were scarce, and Merryck was ten minutes behind time when he arrived at Grenley's house. Ian Hume, sitting in a car parked beside the dusty gardens in the middle of the square, watched him ring the bell with some relief. General Bothwell had been furious at Merryck's unexpected departure, and Hume was under strict orders to collect him when he left Grenley's house and bring him back to the flat.

Merryck, angry with himself for being late, was too preoccupied to bother about possible watchers. He apologized as soon as Grenley opened the door. 'I misjudged the time and the traffic's awful.'

'It's of no consequence. I'm glad you made it all right,' Grenley said.

Merryck followed him upstairs. 'Drawing-room's on the first floor,' Grenley explained. 'Typical of these Kensington squares, and not terribly convenient. Luckily I've a couple who live in the basement and take care of the place.' He led the way into the drawing-room. 'But it's their day off, so we're on our own.'

Fixing drinks, Grenley talked casually, amiably. It could have been an ordinary social occasion, though Merryck was unusually silent. Then Grenley grew serious. 'It's clear you're all right, Hugh, but I gather you've had trouble. Tell me.'

Merryck described the incident in Piccadilly and the destruction of the rooming-house in Marylebone. 'Of course, it could all have been coincidence. But that doesn't seem very likely.'

'What possible reason would the GDR have for wanting you dead at this stage?' Grenley asked.

'God knows!' said Merryck. He sipped the whisky, and then he added, 'Anyway, that's not the first point. Last night I met General Bothwell –'

Grenley's brow puckered into a quick frown. He said sharply, 'You've talked to Bothwell? Spoken to him yourself?'

'Yes,' said Merryck.

'Well, what did you tell him? Did you mention me – or the Office?'

'In connection with the assignment, no.'

'You're quite sure? You gave him no hint?'

'Quite sure, Colin.' Merryck was curt. 'I've not told the General, nor anyone else. I've stuck to the cover story, just as you said. But –'

'Of course you have. I'm sorry, Hugh.' The tension had gone out of Colin Grenley. He got to his feet and held out his hand for Merryck's glass. 'Let me top that while you tell me about Bothwell's ideas. Then we can consider the more serious matter of your future.'

Merryck kept it brief. As he spoke he saw no sign of emotion on Grenley's face other than a mild amusement, and he found himself relaxing. Colin Grenley laughed as Merryck came to an end.

'Trust the General to be logical,' he said. 'It fits, doesn't it? A perfect scenario. And so right.'

It was a split second before the full implication of Grenley's words hit Merryck. Then, 'Right?' he said. He stopped. He gave Grenley a long, hard look. He saw, not the man he'd admired and trusted, but a stranger. 'You mean that –'

'– that I was the so-called traitor, the one who prevented Meissener's defection – and almost Otto Krasner's? That's what you've been thinking, isn't it?' Grenley shook his head. 'No, my dear Hugh. Not me. I was in London at the time and knew nothing about the affair till it was all over.'

'Then why –' Merryck began, and stopped again. His tongue felt thick, and even to himself his voice sounded slurred. But he knew he wasn't drunk. He'd eaten well in the middle of the day – his mother had seen to that – and he'd had only the two whiskies since. Admittedly they'd been strong, especially the second, but . . . The bastard had put something in the liquor. Poison? A narcotic? Some rapid-acting tranquillizer? But why? Why, if he wasn't the traitor?

Merryck passed the back of his hand across his brow. He needed air. He stood up, staggering slightly. Grenley paid him no attention. There was the sound of quick footsteps on the stairs and an elegant woman hurried into the room.

'Julia! What is it?' Grenley said.

Lady Dencourt flung Merryck a bitter look. 'He didn't come alone,' she said. 'He brought watchers. There are two of them outside in a car.'

'Are you sure?'

'Positive.' Then, 'Karl!' she called, and Merryck felt only the smallest jolt of surprise when Duffel Coat came into the room and took up a position inside the door. 'There's no one at the back,' Karl said.

Grenley swung round to Merryck. 'Who are they? Bothwell's men?'

Merryck didn't answer; it was pointless to say he had no idea. The main thing was it didn't seem to have occurred to them that he might be armed. Or perhaps they'd misjudged the effects of the drug. Anyway, he'd managed to move behind a high-backed chair, his pistol concealed but ready, though he doubted his ability to shoot accurately. He braced himself against the chair, his body growing unresponsive, his mind lethargic. He knew he must act soon, while he still could.

'Mein Herr,' the East German said to Grenley, 'if you've got all the information you need from him, we should take him now.'

'Take me where?' said Merryck thickly. If he was to be moved and he could keep awake, he might have a chance to escape.

It was Julia Dencourt who answered, a measure of contempt in her voice. 'You wanted Colin to get you a job, Mr Merryck. Well, he's found you one – one that'll confuse Bothwell and your CIA friends. You're about to defect to the German Democratic Republic – to the USSR later perhaps. There you'll be able to do us no harm. Karl here will go with you. The West's getting a little hot for him. The car's waiting?'

'*Ja.* It is ready.'

'Then go at once,' Julia Dencourt ordered. She was standing at the window, looking through a gap in the curtains at the square below. 'One of the watchers is standing on the pavement. He could be stretching his legs, but he could be coming here. Be quick, Karl.'

'*Ja.*'

It wasn't a moment for hesitation, and Merryck didn't hesitate. After he had killed the hostage his superiors had judged that Captain Merryck could never again be trusted to respond instantly. Now he proved them wrong. His gun came up and he fired.

The East German was equally quick. As Merryck moved an automatic seemed to materialize in the GDR man's hand, and the thump from its silencer was an instant echo of the crack from Merryck's pistol. The effects were startling.

Merryck's shot caught Karl in the shoulder, twisting him

round so that the East German's aim was deflected. His bullet, instead of hitting Merryck, bored a neat round hole between Colin Grenley's eyes and, as Julia Dencourt cut off a scream, Grenley fell backwards. Merryck fired again, wildly, for the drug was beginning to give him double vision, and this time his bullet shattered the beautiful icon that Grenley had recently bought from the art dealer, Svensen.

Through gathering mists Merryck heard the front doorbell begin to ring, and Julia Dencourt's cry, 'Damn you! Damn you! You've ruined everything!' At the same time he saw the East German's gun hand swivel round towards him. He thought he heard the soft thud as Karl pulled the trigger. Instinctively he threw himself sideways, but by now his reactions were much too slow. The bullet caught him in the chest.

Ian Hume heard the first sound of gunfire – the crack of Merryck's pistol – and knew it for what it was: trouble. Snapping some instructions to his driver, he dashed across the road and up the steps to Grenley's front door. He put a finger on the bell and kept it there.

There was a brief interval. Then, as he was contemplating breaking into the house through an area window, the front door was flung open. A woman he recognized as Julia Dencourt stood before him. Her hair was slightly dishevelled, as if she'd run her hands through it, but she was fully in control of herself.

'Yes?' she said calmly.

'I heard shots,' Hume said. 'I –'

'Yes,' she repeated. 'We've had a madman here. He's just killed my fiancé – and a visitor. He escaped through the back. I've called the police.'

'May I?' Ian Hume stepped past her into the hall.

'Who are you?' she demanded.

'You could say I am the police,' Hume replied. He took the stairs two at a time, aware that she was following behind him. He saw Grenley's body and drew a sharp breath. And

Merryck? There, behind that chair. Hume knelt beside him. There was no discernible pulse, but he thought he felt a faint heartbeat.

'He's alive,' Hume said, 'but only just,' and he looked up into Julia Dencourt's cold, hostile face. Seconds later, as the first sirens turned into the square, he heard the front door slam.

For three or four days Merryck hovered between consciousness and unconsciousness in a narrow hospital bed. People came and went. Some were real – doctors, nurses, his family, Ian Hume. Some were wraiths from the recent past: Otto Krasner and Martha; Colin Grenley and Julia Dencourt, the truly distant strangers.

Merryck, though sedated and immobile, was capable of intermittent thought. A great deal he worked out for himself. Between them Grenley and the Dencourt woman had played him for a sucker as part of a complex operation. He'd been hired to find Krasner and lead the GDR killers to him – and to his memoirs. The GDR authorities had to be certain that his memoirs wouldn't compromise a most valuable asset – Julia Dencourt – nor, through her, a network that presumably included Grenley as one of its most influential and accomplished agents in place. And Krasner had to be silenced forever, just in case some trick of memory came to present a future danger. As an added bonus, his death would prove that important defectors remained vulnerable, even after a quarter of a century.

During his first day out of intensive care and in a room of his own Merryck surfaced to find Ian Hume standing at the bottom of the bed, smiling. 'Julia?' Merryck said, the word reflecting his thoughts.

'They caught her,' Hume said. 'She's under interrogation, and we've learnt a good deal already. She was recruited thirty-odd years ago – how isn't yet clear – and directed to marry Sir Francis. It was a good bet on the GDR's part; someone like Sir Francis wasn't likely to keep many secrets from his young, sexy wife. A little pillow-talk and she'd have all she wanted. In the years since Dencourt died she's developed into one of their major controllers.'

'And Grenley?' said Merryck.

'A university recruit, like so many others. He and Julia made a particularly good team – a team with immense prospects, if it hadn't been for you, Hugh.'

'And now?' Merryck asked.

Ian Hume hesitated. 'There's to be a cover-up. It's been announced that Colin Grenley died of a heart attack. As I said, Julia's in custody right now, and answering questions – reluctantly but usefully. The idea seems to be to exchange her for one of our chaps in the GDR. Maybe, as far as the public's concerned, she'll go abroad for an extended holiday and be quietly forgotten. Or that's what our masters'll hope.' Hume couldn't contain his cynicism.

'It must have been a blow to the GDR to learn that Krasner had survived,' Merryck said ruminatively.

'Indeed. They had to mount an operation immediately. They used Grenley, a phone number in a safe house – and you.' Hume looked at Merryck and grinned. 'It's all right,' he said. 'No one's blaming you, Hugh. In fact, General Bothwell's so impressed with your performance he's prepared to offer you a job with his outfit, if you want it – a permanent job.'

'Need you ask?' said Merryck. 'That's great!' After a moment he added, 'I still don't understand why the GDR let me come back to the UK and then tried to dispose of me.'

'They always intended to kill you,' Hume said. 'You put Grenley at risk. They had to get rid of you to ensure his safety. They couldn't know when you might let something slip, or add three and three and make six. But – and it was an important but – Grenley wanted to hear the full story first. Sure, they had a copy of Krasner's memoirs, but only you had actually questioned him and might know if he'd told the CIA anything more. As for the mechanics, we think Grenley must have given the signal for an attack on you as soon as you left his club. Fortunately, the GDR were anxious to avoid any sort of public scandal, and took great care to make sure your death should seem like an accident, so they didn't just shoot to kill. When they'd tried twice and failed, they decided to abduct you – turn you into a defector – which would have made anything you might have let slip, to me, for instance, suspect. But you stopped that, too.'

Merryck smiled weakly. 'So –'

'So all's well – and more than well.'

There was a knock on the door, and Ian Hume called, 'Come in.'

Martha stood there.

'Hugh,' she said. 'You talked about me when you were semi-conscious, and your General phoned –'

Merryck grinned. 'It's good to see you, darling, but –'

'But, nothing! Here I am and here I stay – as long as you want me.'

Merryck drew a deep breath and winced as the wound in his chest stabbed. 'It sounds just fine,' he said.

THE TWISTED TREE

Palma Harcourt

In the bestselling tradition of Helen MacInnes

'Palma Harcourt's novels are spendid' Desmond Bagley

Rescued from an appalling death in the West African state of Korandi, journalist Leo Cantley discovers that the villians may be very different from those the British Government claims responsible – and uncomfortably close to home.

'Palma Harcout writes some of the most satisfactorily difficult to unravel thrillers, and her latest, THE TWISTED TREE, is as good as ever' *SHE magazines*

'THE TWISTED TREE is a cracker' *Daily Telegraph*

'Lots of neat twists against a nicely drawn West African background' Yorkshire Post

'The complexities and subtle unravelling of the plot make this a novel to read at a sitting' *Illustrated London News*

FUTURA PUBLICATIONS
FICTION/THRILLER
0 7088 2461 7

SHADOWS OF DOUBT

Palma Harcourt

In the bestselling tradition of Helen MacInnes

'Palma Harcourt's novels are splendid' Desmond Bagley

Colonel Alexei Bonalov of the KGB approaches a British
Intelligence officer stationed in Moscow with a request
for asylum. As bait, he brings some top secret NATO
documents. Genuine defector or Soviet plant? As the
action moves from Moscow to Paris to London the world
of espionage and counter-espionage is chillingly revealed
as a shadow land where motives are very far from being
clear-cut.

'Nicely tailored spy-fi . . . Philbyesque echoes and cliff-
hanging finish' *Guardian*

'An exciting, fast-moving, readable book' *Financial Times*

'Miss Harcourt is extremely skilfully' *Daily Telegraph*

'What every woman (and many men) needs to know
about espionage' *The Times*

FUTURA PUBLICATIONS
FICTION/THRILLER
0 7088 2462 5

THE BLACK MARBLE
Joseph Wambaugh

Detective Sergeant A. M. Valnikov is a Los Angeles cop who has just seen too much killing. Now he's lost in a haze of vodka and bitter memories.

Natalie Zimmerman is given the job of pulling him back together. A tough, attractive and uncompromising policewoman, she's not keen to share a beat with a man she despises – and one she thinks is half insane.

Together, the ill-assorted couple stumble into a bizarre and brutal extortion case that hurtles the reader through Joseph Wambaugh's most ferociously comic, explosive and surprising novel yet.

'Fast and fascinating' *Daily Telegraph*

'Natural, strong, seductive storytellers aren't a dime a dozen, and Wambaugh's one of them . . . terrific' *Kirkus Reviews*

FUTURA PUBLICATIONS
FICTION
0 7088 1390 9

THE CHOIRBOYS

Joseph Wambaugh

'A STARK UNRELENTING ORGIASTIC BLACK COMEDY . . . a brilliant work of fiction and Wambaugh's finest book to date.' *Los Angeles Times*

A profane, brutal, bitterly funny account of ten cops, working the nightwatch out of Wiltshire Division in Los Angeles. Off duty they attend 'choir practice', an euphemism for the orgies of drink, food and sex that help them escape the emotional torture of police work. Until one night the wild brawl leads to a tragedy that puts an end to choir practice . . . forever.

'IT'S AS THOUGH CATCH-22 HAD BEEN WRITTEN BY POPEYE DOYLE . . . very little in Wambaugh's first two novels prepares one for the scabrous humour and ferocity of THE CHOIRBOYS.' *New York Times*

FUTURA PUBLICATIONS
FICTION
0 8600 7432 3